O. L. Spencer

The Life of Henry Chichelé, archbishop of Canterbury, founder of All Souls College, in the University of Oxford

O. L. Spencer

The Life of Henry Chichelé, archbishop of Canterbury, founder of All Souls College, in the University of Oxford

ISBN/EAN: 9783743337442

Manufactured in Europe, USA, Canada, Australia, Japa

Cover: Foto ©Raphael Reischuk / pixelio.de

Manufactured and distributed by brebook publishing software (www.brebook.com)

O. L. Spencer

The Life of Henry Chichelé, archbishop of Canterbury, founder of

All Souls College, in the University of Oxford

THE

LIFE

OF

HENRY CHICHELÉ,

ARCHBISHOP OF

CANTERBURY,

FOUNDER OF ALL SOULS COLLEGE,

IN THE UNIVERSITY OF OXFORD.

———

LONDON:

PRINTED FOR J. WALTER, CHARING-CROSS.

———

M.DCC.LXXXIII.

TO THE

WARDEN AND FELLOWS

OF

ALL SOULS COLLEGE,

THIS

LIFE OF THE FOUNDER,

IS INSCRIBED,

WITH GRATITUDE AND RESPECT,

BY

THEIR OBLIGED,

HUMBLE SERVANT,

O. L. SPENCER,

FELLOW OF THAT SOCIETY.

PREFACE.

OF the Life which is the subject of the following pages the earliest account extant is to be found in the Statute Book of All Souls College, in the possession of his Grace the Archbishop of Canterbury; from which it has been copied into the Statute Book belonging to the warden of the college. Neither the date of this little treatise, nor the name of the author, is mentioned. A

passage

paffage in it, implying that it was drawn up foon after the fuppreffion of the monafteries, has given occafion to afcribe it to Dr. Warner, warden of the college in the reigns of Henry VIII. Edward VI. and Elizabeth : but the grofs errors with which it abounds will hardly permit us to lay any great ftrefs upon a conjecture, which attributes it to a perfon whofe fituation neceffarily gave him opportunities of obtaining more accurate information. Another account of the fame life was written not many years later than this, fubject, though in a lefs degree, to all the objections which affect the former : it is fhort, incorrect, and unfatisfactory : the author was Robert Hoveden, warden of the college from 1571 to 1614.

THE

THE defects of these superficial sketches have been amply compensated by a work of a very different cast, " The life of archbishop Chichelé, by Arthur Duck, fellow of the college and doctor of civil and canon laws," published in 1617. In compiling this work he has drawn his materials from the best authorities both in print and manuscript.

THE industry and discernment with which he has collected these materials, and the perspicuity with which he has arranged them, have rendered that task, which his very concise mention of Chichelé's earlier years, and his almost total silence respecting the spirited opposition of that prelate to the usurpations of Martin V. seemed to require, neither very intricate nor laborious.

THE authors of the Biographia Britannica have likewife given a life of Chichelé, borrowed, with little variation or addition, from that of Duck. From the elevated rank which he held, and the important fcenes in which he was engaged, he has been incidentally mentioned in moft of the hiftories and public records of the age in which he lived. The regifters of the cathedral churches of Salifbury and St. David's, the Harleian manufcripts, thofe in the archiepifcopal palace at Lambeth, and the archives of New College and All Souls, have furnifhed many fupplemental memorials.

FROM thefe fources I have derived whatever information I have been able to communicate in the following fheets.

As

As I made Duck's life the ground-work of my narrative, I have not thought it neceſſary to ſpecify my obligations to him by particular references; but where-ever I have introduced any thing for which I had not the ſanction of his name, I have regularly cited the authority from which I took it.

THE

THE

L I F E

O F

Archbiſhop *CHICHELÉ.*

S E C T I O N I.

IN the hiſtory of a life extenſively
beneficial the moſt minute incidents
obtain a degree of importance. From
contemplating with pleaſure the great
outlines of it, we are naturally led to
take an intereſt in every ſubordinate cir-
cumſtance ; and we feel a ſenſible diſap-

B pointment,

Sᴇᴄᴛ. I. pointment, if events fo indifferent as the genealogy of a family, or the date of a birth, cannot be afcertained with pre- cifion.

In thefe two articles, however remote- ly connected with his perfonal character, it is to be regretted, that the memorials relating to HENRY CHICHELÉ are not fo full and explicit, as we find them in the more advanced parts of his life.

We are not, however, entirely def- titute of information upon thefe ar- ticles. Higham-ferrers, the place of the Archbifhop's nativity, had been the re- fidence of the Chichelés for more than two generations (*a*). Thomas, his fa-

(*a*) Harleian MSS, N° 1408, pag. 61, 62.

3   ther,

ther, was at leaſt the ſecond in deſcent
after their ſettlement in that town. His
mother, Agnes, was a gentleman's daughter of the name of Pyncheon (*b*). As
no mention is made of any landed property ſo early in the family, an alliance
thus creditable furniſhes a preſumption
that the immediate anceſtor of Henry
had been enabled to make proviſion for
his children by the emoluments of ſome
reputable trade. Of three ſons two raiſed
themſelves by their induſtry to offices of
the higheſt truſt and dignity in the metropolis of the kingdom (*c*). Robert, a
grocer, lived to be choſen twice mayor,

(*b*) Ibid. The Pyncheons bore arms, or, a bend,
three plates with a border counterchanged azure and
ſable. See pref. to Stemmata Chichel. p. viii.

(*c*) Fabian's Chron. p. 386, 388.

arrived

SECT. I. arrived at the honourable diſtinction of
knighthood, and at his death bequeathed
a large portion of a very plentiful for-
tune to charitable uſes. William, in
the ſame line of life, bore the office of
ſheriff and obtained the rank of alder-
man.

THESE deſtinations, and that of Henry, are hardly conſiſtent with the proſpect of hereditary wealth : though, at
the ſame time, the ſucceſs with which
they were attended implies an aſſiſtance
derived from no ſcanty ſource.

UPON the whole it may be fairly pre-
ſumed, that his parents were fully in a
capacity to afford his talents every neceſſary ſupport, though unable to advance
him to the elevated ſtation he filled, by the
influence

influence of their own rank or connexions.
This defect the native independence of superior abilities could easily compensate; and we survey him with admiration opening his own way to the highest ecclesiastical dignities.

THE want of more ample materials leaves us at a loss as to the particular day of his birth : but there is sufficient evidence to warrant the placing of it about the sixty-second year of the fourteenth century; since in 1442 he   1362. describes himself as having either completed or entered upon his eightieth year (*d*).

To the grammar school at Winchester, erected by Wykeham as a nursery

(*d*) See Letter to Eugenius 4, in Appendix, N°1.

B 3

Sect. I. to New College in Oxford *(e)*, Chichelé was indebted for the firſt principles of that erudition which qualified him for the difcharge of the moſt honourable and confidential employments in church and ſtate. From this feminary he was by a regular progreſſion removed to New College; and, together with the participation of every other emolument belonging to that fociety, enjoyed the advantage of profecuting, in eafe and retirement, the ſtudy of the civil and canon law, at that time the moſt direct road to advancement.

In the fequeſtered walks of collegiate life little can arife to attract the notice of the public. The recorded bounty of the founder has preferved the knowledge

(*e*) R. Hoveden's MS. Life in the Archives of All Souls College.

of

of one step in Chichelé's academical ca-
reer, as well as of his residence at a subsequent period. In the year 1388 he
received a dividend of thirteen shillings
and four pence as bachelor of laws: in
1390 an augmented allowance of sixteen
pence a week was granted to him, under
a severe fit of illness, during the greater
part of his confinement *(f)*.

It is probable he did not reside in
Oxford long after this event. We find
him in 1392 presented to a living in
the diocese of St. Asaph *(g)*. In 1396
he became rector of St. Stephen's,
Walbrook *(b)*, on the presentation of the
abbot and convent of St. John of Col-
chester. He was in the same year

(f) E Rotulis computi bursar. of New College.
(g) Godwyn de præsulib. vol. i. p. 126.
(b) Newcourt's repert. vol. i. p. 539.

admitted

admitted an advocate in the court of Arches *(i)*. In 1397 he refigned the rectory of St. Stephen's; and, as the arch-deaconry of Dorfet *(k)* appears to have been conferred upon him about this time, we may conclude that he was already engaged in the fervice of his great patron, RICHARD METFORD, bifhop of Salifbury.

METFORD, in the tumultuous reign of Richard II. had been fteadily attached to the royal party; and having fuffered feverely with them in their adverfity, when they recovered their power, was removed from a canonry of Windfor, firft to the bifhopric of Chichefter, and thence to the fee of Salif-

(i) Godwyn, and his Annotator.

(k) Ibid.—This archdeaconry is now in the diocefe of Briftol.

bury.

bury. A canonry of that cathedral ſtands SECT. I, next in the liſt of Chichelé's eccleſiaſtical 1398. promotions *(l)*. He was now doctor of laws, and vicar general to the biſhop in all ſpiritual matters *(m)*.

To the following pieces of preferment he ſucceeded in the order in which they are ſet down. Rectory of Brington, in the dioceſe of Lincoln, by preſentation of W. de Ferrers, Lord Groby *(n)*. Prebend of Nangwyty, in the collegiate church of Aberguilly *(o)*, by collation of Guy de Mona, his predeceſſor in the epiſcopal chair of St. David's. Rectory of Sherſton, by exchange with John Mayland for the

1400.

(l m) Lowth's Life of Wykeham, p. 199.

(n) Hiſt. of Northamptonſhire, vol. i. p. 37. See article Brington, in the hundred of Newbottle.

(o) Tanner's Biblioth. See article Chichelé.

rectory

Sɛcт. I. reƈtory of Melcombe *(p)*; both in the
diocefe of Sarum; to which laft he was
- prefented by the Earl of Worcefter and
Sir Hugh Le'Defpenfer, joint patrons :
the patronage of Melcombe appears to
have been, for that prefentation, in one
1402. Elena Cerne *(q)*, Archdeaconry of Sa-
1403. lifbury : Canonry of Lincoln *(r)*. The
former of thefe dignities he exchanged
with Walter Metford, the bifhop's bro-
1404. ther, within two years, for the chancel-
lorfhip of the cathedral, together with
the annexed living of Odyham in Hamp-
fhire.—Befides thefe benefices, the Pope
had, by a bull of provifion, nominated
him in 1402 to a prebend of Sarum, a
canonry of the conventual church of
Shaftefbury, and a canonry of the col-

(p) E Regift. Medeford Sarum. f. 64,
(q) Ibid.
(r) Tanner's Biblioth. See article Chichley,

legiate

legiate church of Wilton, whenever Sᴇᴄᴛ. I.
they fhould become vacant *(s)*.

How early foever Chichelé might
have been defigned for the church, we
have no authority to date his entrance
upon the ecclefiaftical office earlier than
1392 : he was then ordained fubdea-   1392.
con by the bifhop of Derry *(t)*. He
was admitted to the order of prieft 1396,   1396.
by William bifhop of Bafil *(u)*. From
whom he received ordination as deacon,
is not mentioned. We are equally un-
certain as to the time when he took upon
him the inferior orders : and the infti-
tutions of the church of Rome, owing
to great irregularity and relaxation of
difcipline in the obfervance of them, are

(s) Act. Pub. tom. iv. p. 23.
(t u) Tanner, as above.

                      not

not calculated to affift us in this uncer-
tainty.

OF feven Orders eftablifhed in that
church, three alone, thofe of Subdea-
con, Deacon, and Prieft, were accounted holy. The four inferior, of Porter,
Reader, Exorcift, and Acolyte, though
fcrupuloufly obferved in primitive times,
were gradually become of no other importance to the candidates for the mini-
ftry, than as previous fteps to the three
fuperior orders, and, as fuch, were all
frequently conferred in one day : yet,
by the indulgence of the fame church,
thefe acceffory orders were confidered as
qualifications for ecclefiaftical preferments *(w)*.

(w) Durandi Rationale, lib. ii, cap, 1.   Morinus,
de Grad. Ecclef. par. iii. p, 186.

ODYHAM,

ODYHAM, the laſt benefice Chichelé
enjoyed from the bounty of his protector Metford, was in the diocefe of
Wincheſter. To have received inſtitu-
tion at the hands of the venerable prelate, Wykeham, whofe munificence had
laid the foundation of his fortunes, muſt
have rendered this promotion one of the
moſt pleaſing, though not one of the moſt
important, occurrences in his life: the
recent deceafe of that great and good man
precluded him from this ſatisfaction. His
feelings were put to a feverer trial by
the death of the biſhop of Saliſbury,
with whom he lived in the moſt familiar habits of friendly intercourfe. As
a token of his lateſt regard, the biſhop
bequeathed him a golden goblet with a
cover, and appointed him his principal
executor.

WHAT-

WHATEVER we may allow him to have facrificed on this occafion to the calls of friendfhip, his abilities had acquired a ftrength too firm to fink under the fhock ; and his reputation needed no adventitious fupport. He had been reprefented to his fovereign as a man of a comprehenfive and verfatile genius, corrected by a found and difcerning judgment: and Henry had employed him, firft on an embaffy to Pope Innocent VII. and, in the courfe of the fame year, at the court of France. His commiffions (x), in the former of which Sir John Cheyne, in the latter Cheyne and Mortimer are joined with him, bear date 1406. July 11, and October 8, 1406. In the April following he was again honoured with the public character of embaffa-

(x) Act. Pub. tom. iv. p. 100, 102.

dor

dor to Gregory XII. *(y)* ; a pontiff, of
whom the Italian *(z)* writers have condefcended to record, that, in the expences
of his houfhold, the fingle article of
fugar amounted to more than the food
and raiment of feveral of his predeceffors.

In this embaffy Chichelé acquitted
himfelf fo much to the Pope's fatisfac-
tion, who then held his court at Sienna,
that he received a very fubftantial proof
of his efteem within few weeks after
his arrival. Guy de Mona, bifhop of
St. David's, having deceafed the latter
end of Auguft, the news no fooner
reached the court of Gregory, than he
prefented Chichelé to the vacant fee by

(y) Act. Pub. tom. iv. 113.
(z) Muratori and others; fee Annali d'Italia,
p. 37, tom. ix.

way

way of provifion. There is fome un-
certainty about the time of his confe-
cration *(a)* ; but it is very probable, as
the Pope quitted Sienna *(b)* in the
1408. January enfuing, that Chichelé, who
accompanied him to Lucca, and refided
fome months there in his retinue, was
confecrated early in May the fame year
in that city. He arrived in England
about the middle of Auguft, and. was
invefted by the archbifhop of Canterbury

(a) The regifter of St. David's mentions his con-
fecration as performed on May 17 ; but the *place* and
the *year* are not legible: yet the dates of thofe parts
of the regifter, which are in better prefervation,
correfpond fo uniformly with the date of his confe-
cration there given, that one can hardly doubt its
accuracy. *Duek,* who is in general remarkably cor-
rect, is probably mifinformed when he fays, that
Chichelé was confecrated in October 1407.

(b) Chronicle of Sienna. Murat. coll. tom. xix.
p. 421.

with

with the fpiritualities of his bifhopric on the 26th. Letters patent for the reftitution of his temporalities had, at the pope's folicitation, been made out before his return, under the cuftomary obligation of renouncing every claim prejudicial to the king's prerogative.

To underftand in what manner thefe papal prefentations interfered with the fovereign rights of the crown of England, it may not be improper to take a view of the matter a little more at large. That the catholic church, of which the popes claimed the fole direction and fuperintendence, might not be injured by neglect of fervice, or the appointment of unfit minifters, thefe holy fathers affumed the privilege of difpofing of the moft valuable ecclefiaftical benefices by way of *provifion* : a term originally

C confined

confined to the affignment of a benefice before it became vacant, but applied indifcriminately in procefs of time to any prefentation of the pope. This privilege was collaterally fecured, by the long-eftablifhed cuftom of drawing to their own tribunals every caufe that was in any wife connected with fpiritual matters. Edward III. endeavoured to ftem this torrent of papal encroachments by the ftatutes of provifors and præmunire, which prohibited the fubject from accepting any benefice at the pontiff's hands without the royal licence, and from profecuting any fuit in a foreign court. Thefe ftatutes were revived by Richard II. and continued through this and feveral fucceeding reigns; though ineffectual for the purpofe of reftraining papal ufurpation. The pope ftill afferted his pretenfions, and his provifions took

place :

place: only the claimant under them
was obliged to renounce all title conferred by them to the temporalities, and
every expreffion contained in the bull
that could be conftrued in prejudice of
the crown.

SECTION

SECTION II.

HIS acknowledged talents for ne-gotiation did not allow the new-made bishop of St. David's to go through all the ceremonies that concur to the completion of the episcopal character. He was not yet inthroned when he was 1409. summoned to a synod, called by arch-bishop Arundel, to deliberate upon the choice of proper persons to represent the English nation at the council of Pisa.

THIS council was convened with a view to the settlement of a schism that had divided the Roman church, and dif-graced the apostolic chair, by the double claim of rival pretenders, for more than thirty years. Gregory had been raised

to

to that chair, by one party of pious ſticklers for the integrity of the ſucceſſion of St. Peter, on condition of his reſigning, if, by a general decree of the Chriſtian church, his competitor Benedict ſhould be judged to have the cleareſt title to it.

By the unanimous ſuffrages of the ſynod, Robert Hallum, biſhop of Saliſbury, Thomas Chillingdon, prior of Canterbury, and Chichelé, were deputed to attend the Piſan council : and, to defray their expences, every beneficed clergyman was taxed in the proportion of four pence in the pound for all his ecclefiaſtical poſſeſſions. The ſpiritual envoys took their journey through France, and in their progreſs were ſplendidly entertained by the univerſity of Paris, and treated with every other mark of the moſt flattering attention. On the

C 3

the 27th of April they arrived at Pisa, and were witnesses to the deposition of Gregory and the antipope Benedict, both of whom had acted a very subtle and disingenuous part through the whole business. On the 7th of July the cardinals made their election of the archbishop of Milan, who, on his accession to the papal throne, took upon him the name of Alexander V. His history is short and singular. He was by birth a Cretan. His parents have not been so clearly ascertained. Thrown young upon the world, he sustained for a time the hardships of a vagabond life and precarious subsistence: till a Minorite friar, touched with his distress, and observing in him symptoms of a genius that promised to repay the cultivation, removed him to the friendly shelter of a convent, and the comforts of a regular provision. Having procured him admission

admiffion into his own order, he in-
ftructed him in the elements of grammar and logic, the prevailing ftudies
of the age. On this bafis Alexander
raifed a fuperftructure of extenfive erudition. Having applied himfelf clofely
to ethics and divinity at Oxford, and
read lectures in thofe fciences with great
reputation at Paris, he was in the courfe
of few years promoted to the fee of
Milan. This poft he filled when the
fentence of the conclave pronounced him
the legitimate fucceffor of St. Peter; a
ftation to which he brought the rare
qualifications of profound learning and
incorruptible fimplicity of manners; but
he brought them allayed by the indolence of monaftic habits, and the love
of literary eafe. The vexations of a
life repugnant to his natural bent of
mind operating on the ordinary infir-

mities

mities of age *(a)* once more vacated
the apoftolic chair within the revolu-
tion of twelve months *(b)* : if that
chair could with propriety be termed
vacant, to which Gregory and Benedict
perfifted in avowing their claim.

CHICHELE' did not remain long in
Italy after Alexander's inauguration.
He returned to England in the winter
of the fame year; and, refuming his paftoral cares, diligently applied himfelf
to a confcientious difcharge of them,
during a refidence of feveral months *(c)*.

(a) John XXIII. was fufpected of having contributed to his death by poifon. L'Enfant. Hift. de
concile de Conftance, Liv. ii. chap. 77 : but
his death was more probably the natural effect of
age.

(b) Bower's Lives of the Popes, vol. vii.
p. 123.

(c) Regifter of St. David's.

I T

IT is to this period that we muſt re-
fer a propoſal from him of reſigning certain preferments, which he held in com-
mendam, if he might be permitted to
preſent to them; a requeſt that the pope
and the king made no difficulty of
granting *(d)*. The latter end of May
he was again ſent to France with Sir
John Cheyne, Cattryck, and Henry Lord
Beaumont, to negotiate a renewal of the
truce between the two kingdoms. By
letters dated December 23d, the objeᶜt
of their negotiation appears to have been
happily effeᶜted : but the jealouſies of
the borderers made it neceſſary to inveſt
the commiſſioners with freſh powers the
year following, for the ſettlement of
ſome ſubſequent infraᶜtions *(e)*. After
the adjuſtment of this affair Chichelé

(d) (e) Aᶜt. Pub. tom. iv. p. 171.

reviſited

Sᴇcт. revifited his diocefe, and was inthroned
II. May the 11th with the ufual ceremonies *(f)*.

In this and the next year we find him
frequently refident at his epifcopal pa-
1412. lace, and an adjoining manor *(g)*. In one
of thefe vifits to his diocefe he collated
William Chichelé to a prebend in his
cathedral *(h)*, probably the elder fon of
his brother William ; who, it appears,
was bred a clergyman, attained confiderable preferment in the church, and died
at Rome on an embaffy to the pope *(i)*.
From the dates of his injunctions within the laft eighteen months *(k)* we
may collect, that he refided at intervals

(f) Regifter of St. David's,
(g) *(h)* Ibid.
(i) Pref. to Stemm. Chichel. p. 1c.
(k) Regifter of St. David's.

in

in the metropolis, which the death of his royal master foon rendered a scene of more than ordinary business and importance.

HENRY IV. closed the weary course of a turbulent reign on the 20th of March 1413. He had wrested the scep- tre by violence from the hand of the rightful possessor, and maintained it in a hard and doubtful struggle against the most formidable enemies; whose open revolt and hostile defiance subsided only in the suspicious stillness of suppressed resentments and covered treason.

IF the church lost a powerful protector in this prince, they felt no diminution of their authority in the succession of his heir. Henry of Monmouth, while he favoured the interests of the clergy at large, reposed a

particular

particular confidence in Chichelé. The
fpace of very few weeks intervened between the demife of the late, and his
employment under the reigning, fovereign. With the bifhop of Exeter he
was appointed to determine a fuit between the city of Bayonne and one Peter de Conties *(l)*. The circumftances
of this caufe are not upon record; but
the exprefs refervation of the final fentence to the king himfelf implies, that
it was not of a trivial nature.

THERE cannot be produced a more
convincing argument of Chichelé's fuperior fkill in the management of great
political objects, than his repeated public charges. After a very fhort inter-
miffion of national bufinefs, he was
again called out in the fervice of his

(l) Act. Pub. tom. iv. part. 2. p. 31.

country,

country, in conjunction with the Earl of Warwick, Lord Zouch, and other commiffioners, to lay before the court of France fome conditions of treaty ; the chief of which was a renewal of the truce that had fubfifted, with frequent interruptions, from the 20th of Richard II. *(m)*. They had it alfo in their inftructions, to conclude an alliance of perpetual peace with the duke of Burgundy. The former only of thefe was effectuated : and the ratification of a truce for eight months was fignified by letters from the embaffadors, dated September, at Lenlingham *(n)*, a frontier town, and the ufual place of conference. It is evident, from thefe various renewals of the original truce, that the faith of treaties was not very religioufly obferved by

(m) (n) Act. Pub. tom. iv. part 2. p. 40, 41, 48.

either

either party. The possession of the English on the ancient territories of France,
submitted to with impatience, and maintained with captious exactness, admini-
stered perpetual matter for contention.

This was the last political character in
which Chichelé appeared as bishop of
St. David's: in the spring of 1414, he was
translated to the see of Canterbury, vacant by the death of archbishop Arundel.
The prior and monks of that church,
having obtained the king's congé d'élire,
proceeded to make their election : and
the votes being unanimous in favour of
Chichelé, two of the chapter were deputed to acquaint him with their choice,
and to beg his approbation. He was
then in London ; and, on the arrival of
the delegates, having taken a short time
for deliberation, he the next morning,

1414.

I   in

in prefence of the Duke of York and the Bifhop of Norwich, delivered his fentiments to this effect: That, confidering himfelf as united in the bonds of fpiritual matrimony to the church of St. David's, he could not look forward to new engagements till thefe bonds were cancelled by the pope. The prior and brotherhood made immediate application for that purpofe, and their petition was ftrongly feconded by the crown.

Aᴛ once to preferve the honour of the apoftolic fee, and to confult its interefts, required no fmall addrefs. The old papal claim of providing to vacancies in the church could not confiftently be waved: and to offend the Englifh monarch, by an obftinate oppofition to his wifhes, was by no means fafe. A court lefs fruitful in expedients than that of Rome might have been embarraffed how

to

to act in ſo delicate a conjuncture: to obviate every difficulty, a middle plan was adopted: the pontiff inſiſted upon his right of proviſion; but at the ſame time took care to gratify the humour of the petitioners, by providing the perſon of their choice.

CHICHELE' received the pall from the hands of the biſhop of Wincheſter, after having profeſſed obedience to the Pope in the cuſtomary forms. Inveſted with the ſpiritualities he repaired to the king at Leiceſter; and, having prayed the reſtitution of his temporalities, and, formally renouncing every claim under the papal proviſion derogatory from the rights of the crown, was put in full *(o)* poſſeſſion of them May 13th.

As

(*o*) Duck and Godwyn ſay, that Chichelé compounded for the temporalities during the vacancy of
the

As he now begins to move in a more enlarged fphere, it will be requifite to carry our attention back to fome preceding events, on which much of the perfpicuity of the enfuing account muft neceffarily depend.

the fee by a prefent of fix hundred marks. The inftrument of reftitution in the *Acta Publica* takes no notice of this compofition. Chichelé's petition there recited extends to all the iffues and profits of the fee during its vacancy, and the king's proclamation fays only "reftituimus prout moris eft."

SECTION III.

THE spirit of bold speculation and free inquiry, introduced by Wickliffe, and propagated with zeal by his disciples, had, in the two last reigns, made great strides, if not towards weakening the authority of the church, at least in abating the respect paid to it.

THE natural consequence of viewing the sacerdotal order with diminished veneration was a desire to deprive its members of a part of the plentiful revenues they at that time enjoyed; and which seemed the more exorbitant, from being considered as useless defalcations from the general stock. Few years had elapsed since the commons, assembled

in

in parliament, prefented a bill for con-
verting to the relief of the national ne-
ceffities the temporal poffeffions of the
church. Thefe, they alledged *(p)*, would
maintain 15 earls, as many hundred
knights,' 6,000 efquires, 100 new almf-
houfes, and leave a furplus of 20,000
marks for the contingent expences of the
crown. According to their eftimate, the
clergy poffeffed a yearly income of
322,000 *(q)* marks; a fum that muft
have appeared enormous, when the fufficient provifion of a prieft was computed
at the annual ftipend of 7 *(r)* marks.

THE prudence of the king had check-
ed the progrefs of this violent proceed-

(p) Fab. Chron. p. 386.

(q) Ibid. equal to about 214,000 *l.*

(r) Ibid. by the fame computation, the number
of priefts adequate to the fervice of religion throughout England was calculated at 15,000.

ing;

SECT.
III.
ing; but the difpofition which dictated it ftill prevailed.

WE have already feen fome overtures of peace between France and England. The former kingdom had been long har-raffed with the moft cruel inteftine divifions : Charles VI. the reigning monarch, was, from frequent and lafting paroxyfms of infanity, rendered incapable of attending to the government of the realm ; and this rich and populous country was become a facrifice to the factious pride and deep refentments of the two powerful houfes of Orleans and Burgundy.

DELUSIVE hopes of a reconciliation were, for a confiderable time, confidently entertained, and true patriots hailed the aufpicious omen with unfeigned joy;

joy; when, in the year 1412, according to the simple manners of the age, the two dukes were seen riding through the streets of Auxerre, mounted on one horse *(f):* but these flattering appearances were of short duration *(t)*. Henry IV. whose friendship they had alternately solicited, politically fomented their diffension, foreseeing that it must eventually tend to the advantage of his dominions.

SUCH was the relative situation of the kingdom, such the temper of the people,

(f) Villaret's History of France, tom. vii. p. 107.

(t) A French memorialist has ascribed the origin of this quarrel to a very unwarrantable vanity in the duke of Orleans ; who, that he might have the reputation of an intrigue with the duchess of Burgundy, placed her portrait in a cabinet of beauties supposed to have fallen victims to his gallantry. Gollut. Mem. of the House of Burgundy, p. 626.

D 3

when

when Chichelé entered upon the adminiftration of the metropolitan fee ; and
in that capacity became peculiarly engaged in the fupport of the eftablifhed
religion, and the protection of a numerous body of regular and fecular clergy.
He could not have undertaken this
charge at a more critical juncture ; the
parliament, now convened at Leicefter,
revived the old attack upon the temporalities of the church, and warmly exhorted the king to take them into his
own hands. The embaffadors of France
were actually in England, and Henry
had fignified to them demands on their
court, which amounted to little lefs than
an open declaration of hoftilities. In
fuch a pofture of affairs, every propofal
that promifed a fupply could not fail of
being attentively liftened to : and the
king began to confider the meafure fuggefted

gefted to him by his faithful commons as equally convenient and practicable.

This was a dreadful alarm to the clergy; and it required all their prudence to parry a blow aimed fo directly at the vitals of their conftitution. After frequent confultations, they refolved to divert the impending danger, by the voluntary ceffion of a part of their poffeffions. Chichelé undertook to lay this offer before the king in parliament. In a ftudied harangue upon the occafion, he earneftly urged the recovery of Henry's hereditary dominions in France, and fpoke very largely and learnedly upon the falique law. The old chronicles attribute the king's fixed refolution of carrying his arms into France to the influence of this fpeech. It is certain, however, that this refolution was taken pre-

vioufly

viously to Chichelé's oration *(u)*; which seems rather to have been framed, in order to bring the parliament into the king's views. Ralph Neville, earl of Weftmoreland, is said to have oppofed fome articles of this fpeech, affirming that the war fhould commence with Scotland; and to have been fully an-fwered on thefe points by the duke of Exeter; a nobleman who had acquired, in the academies of Italy, a tafte for let-ters very uncommon amongft the laity in this century *(w)*.

If the revenues of the Englifh clergy efcaped, the alien priories were given up without hefitation, and vefted in the

(*u*) See Claims of Henry on the Crown of France, 1413, Acta Pub. and Rapin.

(*w*) Thefe fpeeches are of fufpicious authority, though given by all the old chroniclers.

king

king by parliament ; except fuch as were conventual, or where the power of electing their own head rendered them lefs neceffarily dependent on foreign abbies.

CHICHELE', in concurrence with thefe meafures, confirmed in convocation *(x)* an order of the council, prohibiting any future promotion of a foreigner to fpiritual dignity or benefice, before he had given fecurity that he would neither divulge the fecrets of government, nor in any manner abet the defigns of the enemy. The fame regard to the conftitutional interefts of his own country prompted him to propofe the abolition of all immunities and exemptions granted by authority of the pope *(y)*.

(x) Hollingfhed. tom. ii. p. 547.
(y) Walfingham, Hypod. Heuft. p. 579.

THE

SECT.
III.

1415.

THE spring of 1415 opened with the most unequivocal appearances of a French war. No preparation was neglected that could forward the favourite scheme of invasion. The next object of importance was the administration of the realm during the sovereign's absence. Chichelé, who held the highest rank in the council *(z)* appointed to execute this trust, was invested likewise with the authority to muster *(a)* all the clergy, as well regular as secular, throughout his diocese, for the defence of the coast; a manifest indication, that the kingdom was greatly depopulated by the levies for a continental war. Orders of the same import were sent to most of the other bishops: and the temporal peers

(z) Act. Pub. tom. iv. part 2d. p. 112.
(a) Ibid. ut supra, p. 123.

were

were impowered to raife the militia of the different counties.

We fhall obtain fome flight idea of the quarters that were moft open to incurfion, if we add the difpofition of the regular forces left for home fervice *(b)*. Of thefe, 200 lances and 400 archers were affigned for the guard of the eaft and weft marches towards Scotland ; 100 lances and 200 archers for that of North and South Wales ; and for the fea coaft in general 150 lances, 300 archers, and double fhipping.

The internal defence of England being thus arranged, the king looked forward with the more fecurity to the embarkation of his troops for France :

(b) Act. Pub. tom. iv. part 2d. p. 112.

but

body
SECT.
III.

but he did not engage in this important enterprize unprepared for an event, which the hazardous nature of his expedition rendered neither very improbable, nor perhaps very diftant. In the will, which he executed previoufly to his departure, Chichelé was affectionately remembered, in the bequeft of a crimfon embroidered velvet robe *(c)*.

In this ftate of affairs the French embaffadors returned, to prevent, if poffible, the projected attack, by more ample conceffions on the part of their court. They were feafted at the royal table in the caftle of Winchefter; and Chichelé, by command of the king, having given them a peremptory anfwer, they departed, under fafe conduct, the

(c) Act. Pub. tom. iv. part 2d. p. 138.

unwelcome

unwelcome harbingers of Henry's arrival, who with a formidable army quickly appeared at the gates of Harfleur.

WHEN the whole, almoft, of the lands in England was held by military tenure, we fhall not be furprized to find the pay of the army regulated, in a great meafure, by the civil rank of the perfons who compofed it. But whilft a duke received a mark a day, an earl half a mark, a baron 4 fhillings, and an efquire 2, we fhall be led to conclude very unfavourably of the philofophy and fcience of the age, on finding the fervices of a phyfician rated no higher than at 1 fhilling a day, the eftablifhed wages of a man at arms *(d)*.

THE progrefs of the royal army, and

(d) Act. Pub. tom. iv. part 2d. p. 112. 116.

the

the glorious day of Azincourt, are too well known to need a particular defcription. To the trophies that crowned the victorious furvivors of that hard-fought field I find a fingular privilege added, and confirmed in the year 1417 by an act *(e)*, which forbade any perfon to wear a coat of arms, without hereditary right, or gift of lands to which arms belonged, unlefs he had fought at the battle of Azincourt; a title deemed equivalent to every other.

To return to the archbifhop; in conformity to his prince's commands, he enjoined all the ecclefiaftics in the diocefe of Canterbury to hold themfelves in readinefs to repell the enemy, if they made any incurfions on that coaft.

(e) Act. Pub. tom. iv. part 2d. p. 201.

T h e

THE king revisited England in November; and Chichelé, on the 28th of
the same month, summoned a provincial
synod at London. The first day was
devoted to the duties of religion. The
archbishop performed mass at the great
altar of St. Paul's. On the succeeding
days, the upper and lower houses of
convocation went into a discussion of
ecclesiastical matters; and having decreed two tenths to be paid, within two
years, towards the support of the war,
and commanded the religious observance
of the anniversaries of St. David, St.
Chad, St. Winifred, and St. George,
the archbishop dissolved the assembly.

IT was during this synod that Chichelé, together with the bishops of
Winchester and Durham, and Sir John
Rotherhale, was appointed to receive all
the

SECT.
III.

the profits arising from wardfhips, and marriages of wards of the crown, and to apply them to the expences of the king's voyage *(f)*.

1416.

ANOTHER convocation was affembled by Chichelé on the firft of April following, to deliberate about the nomination of frefh delegates for the council of Conftance *(g)*; which the death of fome

(f) Act. Pub. tom. iv. part 2d. p. 150.

(g) The depofition of John XXIII, who was accufed of every crime that fhocks and difgraces human nature; the confirmation of the practice, which had prevailed in the Roman church about two centuries, of giving the *laity* the facrament only in one kind, left (amongft other reafons) they might defile the cup by dipping their long beards in; and the firft admiffion of the Englifh on an equal foot with France, Italy, Germany, and Spain, which hitherto had enjoyed the exclufive privilege of being ftyled *nations* by the court of Rome; were no inconfiderable part of the bufinefs that occupied the fathers of the council of Conftance, from its commencement 1413, to its diffolution 1417.

who

who had been fent thither two years before, and the increafed number of agents
from other courts, made neceffary. The
bifhop of London, twelve doctors, and
the chancellors of the two univerfities,
were named to anfwer this requifition;
and their expences were defrayed, as
ufual, by an affeffment on the church.
In the fame meeting the rapid advances
of heretical doctrines became a fubject of
alarming confideration; as we may infer
from a conftitution for the repreffion of
them, publifhed by Chichelé in the
fummer of the current year.

ABOUT this period the emperor Si-
gifmund vifited England, and, in conjunction with the French embaffadors,
endeavoured to effect a peace between
the two belligerant powers. But the
news of the fiege of Harfleur under the

E   direction

direction of the constable Armagnac, in-
terrupted the negotiations; and the king,
having defpatched the duke of Bedford
to fuccour the befieged, after a fhort interval accompanied the emperor on his
road to Conftance as far as Calais.

HITHER Chichelé, having brought
the fynod to a conclufion, followed his
fovereign; and at the head of a delegacy
appointed to treat with the archbifhop
of Rheims and others, on the old and
unpromifing bufinefs of peace, accom-
plifhed the fecondary object of a four
months truce *(b)*, to be obferved by land
through the marches of Picardy and all
weftern Flanders, and by fea from Mo-
rocco to Norway.

(b) Act. Pub. tom. iv. part 2d. p. 179.

DURING

_ DURING the abode of the Englifh court at Calais, king Henry had an interview with the duke of Burgundy; on which occafion Gloucefter, the king's brother, became an hoftage to count Charolois, the duke of Burgundy's fon; at whofe firft vifit, as a contemporary *(i)* writer of credit has obferved with fome refentment, the Englifh prince, inftead of advancing to meet him, continued feveral moments in difcourfe with his domeftics, and at length, making him only a flight bow, added coldly, " Fair " coufin, welcome."

LATE in November Chichelé returned in the king's train to England, and, having fummoned, by his order, an affembly of the clergy at London, obtained

(i) Monftrelet, chap. clxi. vol. 1.

E 2   a grant

a grant of two tenths for the profecution of the war *(k)*; and fettled the annual celebration of the feafts of St. Crifpin and St. John of Beverley : the latter of thefe faints was believed to have taken an uncommon intereft in the toils of the combatants at Azincourt, his tomb having been remarked by fome devout pilgrims to have diftilled large drops of oil during that bloody conflict. The injunction for the obferving of thefe feafts, dated at the archbifhop's manor of Otteford *(l)*, clofes this year.

(k) Act. Pub. tom. iv. part 2d. p. 189.

(l) The manor of Otteford was exchanged by archbifhop Warham with Henry VIII. continued in the crown till the time of the civil war ; was then granted to colonel Robert Gibbons, and is now in the Leicefter family.—Philpot, and Harris's Survey of Kent.—Phil. pag. 263. Har. 238.

SECTION

S E C T I O N IV.

THE king, whofe thoughts were wholly fixed upon the French war, embarked for Normandy the latter end of the fummer; and, on his departure, Chichelé ordered prayers to be offered up in all the churches throughout his province, for the fafety of his royal perfon, and a bleffing on his arms. In December he held a convocation at London, in which the clergy, at his inftance, granted the king a further fum of two tenths. At this fynod the interefts of the univerfity of Oxford became a principal topic of debate. Robert Gilbert, warden of Merton College, in an elegant and mafterly fpeech expatiated upon the deplorable condition that feat

E 3   of

of learning was reduced to : where thofe candidates for preferment, who had qualified themfelves by a long courfe of ftudy, were too frequently fuffered to languifh in neglect and obfcurity within the narrow verge of their college walls; while adventurers of lefs experience in the fields of fcience obtained rewards due only to the perfevering virtue of veterans. To remove a grievance that appeared to be equally the lot of the fifter univerfity, Chichelé publifhed a conftitution, decreeing, that in the future difpofal of ecclefiaftical benefices regard fhould be had to the academical rank of the candidate; and the value of the living conferred be in proportion to the proficiency of the prefentee. The falutary effects of this decree were defeated, for the prefent, by the jealous obftinacy of the lower order of graduates;

who

who, when the queftion came to be SECT.
formally agitated before the univerfi- IV.
ties, were by their fuperior numbers 1417.
enabled to reject it; willing to lofe every
beneficial effect of this conftitution, rather than be inftrumental to the advancement of any members of their own body
in preference to themfelves.

In the fame affembly Chichelé announ-
ced the election of the cardinal Colonna to
the government of the catholic church.
The fchifm which had long impaired
the authority of the papal fee was now
finally terminated; and Martin V. (for
that was the title affumed by the new
pontiff) was not of a temper to neglect
any advantages which the plenary domi-
nion revived in his perfon offered to his
ambition. He in two years filled 13
bifhoprics in the province of Canterbury by provifion.

E 4 BEFORE

BEFORE the archbifhop difmiffed the
fynod he gave a mandate to the dean
and chapter of St. Paul's to denounce,
in the moft public manner, a folemn anathema againft certain perfons unknown,
who had murdered three priefts within
the fanctuary of that cathedral. And
that no formality might be wanting to
give it weight, the bells were to be toll-
ed, and the burning tapers ufed in the
ceremony caft on the ground and trampled under foot, at the delivery of the
awful fentence *(a)*. A tranfaction of a
lefs favage complexion, but attended
with

(a) An eye-witnefs of the fact mentions a fimilar
form of excommunication obferved at the reconciliation of the emperor Frederick I. and pope Alexander III. in the church of St. Mark at Venice. The
pope ordered lighted tapers to be given to the emperor, the clergy, and the laity prefent, and then
pronounced this anathema, " In the name of God,
the bleffed Virgin, the holy apoftles Peter and Paul,
and

with very aggravating circumftances, had
called for Chichelé's animadverfion in
the preceding fpring. Lord Strange
having, at the inftigation of his wife,
entered into a difpute with Sir John
Truffel, had wreaked his refentment by
an open attack on him in St. Dunftan's
church during the performance of divine
fervice; and a citizen, named Petwardin,
had in the affray fallen a facrifice to his
friendly interpofition. The archbifhop,
upon a full inveftigation of the matter,
fentenced Lord Strange to walk through
the public ftreets, from St. Paul's cathe-

and all the faints, we cut off from the bofom of the
church all who fhall dare to infringe this peace,
and, as thefe tapers are extinguifhed, fo may their
fouls be deprived of the light of eternal vifion." Then
the tapers being caft on the floor and trampled under
foot, the emperor cried out " Amen."

Romualdo of Salerno. See
Muratori's Collect. of Italian Writers, tom. viii.
p. 239, 240.

dral

dral to St. Dunſtan's church, bearing in his hand a wax taper of a pound weight; and, as a further mark of his contrition, to offer in the ſacred edifice he had polluted a pyx of ſilver gilt. His lady, in addition to the humiliating taſk of accompanying her lord in the ſame penitential manner, was at the purification of the church compelled to fill with her own hands the water veſſels employed on the occaſion, and to preſent at the altar an ornament worth ten pounds. So mortifying an atonement made by perſons of exalted rank is no trifling evidence of the force of eccleſiaſtical cenſures at this æra *(b)*.

Since his arrival in France Henry had made rapid advances towards the

(b) Hollingſhed, vol. ii. p. 562 ; and Wilkin's Concilia, vol. iii. p. 385.

reduction

reduction of Normandy. In September his army was occupied in the fiege of Rouen ; where, after a regular vifitation of the diocefe of Rochefter, and the appointment of a vicar general during his abfence, Chichelé joined the Englifh camp.

WHEN the calamities of war are mitigated by the generous fpirit of chivalry, the detail of martial fcenes becomes lefs grating to the humane ear. In their march to Pont de l'Arche, a fmall but advantageous poft in Normandy, a detachment of Englifh had orders to pafs a part of the Seine. " To-morrow," fays Cornwall, their gallant leader, to the captain of a petty fortrefs on the oppofite bank, " to-morrow I pafs the river, " and you fhall pay my paffage with the " beft charger in your ftables: if I hold
" not

" not my word, my cap of steel shall
" answer the forfeit, but it shall cost
" you five hundred French nobles."
The challenge was accepted, and Cornwall gained the pass the next morning.

A TREATY at this time in agita-
tion made Chichelé's presence the more
necessary in France. The proposals
however of a young monarch flushed
with conquest were not of a nature to
succeed, even under the direction of the
ablest negotiator. Cardinal Ursini, who
acted as mediator between the two courts,
endeavoured to soften Henry in his demands, by shewing him the portrait of
the French princess, Catherine *(c)*. His
heart was not insensible to the attractions of beauty, but he had ambition

(c) Monstrelet, chap. 193.

above

above the control of any rival paffion. At a fubfequent conference near Meulan the queen, at her firft vifit, brought the princefs with her. This interview confirmed the favourable impreffion Henry had received from the fight of her portrait, without inducing him to abate a fingle article of his pretenfions on the crown of France. Finding the conceffions on the part of that crown by no means anfwerable to his expectations, he faid angrily to the duke of Burgundy, " Fair coufin, be it known " to you, that I am determined to have " your fovereign's daughter, and all that " I have demanded with her, or to " drive both him and you out of his do- " minions *(d)*."

(d) Monftrelet, chap. 200. 207.

THE

SECT. IV.

1418.

THE siege of Rouen was still prosecuted with unremitting efforts, and the defence as vigorously maintained. Being reduced to extremity, the besieged sent to their king and the duke of Burgundy for succours; and remonstrated on the scandalous neglect they had experienced with a freedom and sharpness highly characteristic of their determined courage. "If," said they, "we are driven to the "harsh necessity of surrendering to the "arms of England, the feeble govern- "ment that is unable to afford us pro- "tection shall find in us the fierceft and "most implacable enemies *(e)*." Their remonstrance was ineffectual : all the calamities of famine and war were sustained with the most invincible fortitude; nor did the garrison make any overtures of capitulation, till above fifty thousand

(e) Monstrelet, chap. 200.

of

of the inhabitants had perished by hun-
ger and difeafe. A herald at length entered the Englifh camp, and demanded
a fafe conduct for fix perfons, two of
the church, two gentlemen, and two of
inferior rank. Henry, irritated by their
obftinate valour, would at firft liften to
nothing fhort of unconditional fubmif-
fion. In the eyes of men who had already made fo noble a ftand in defence of
their liberties; any event appeared pre-
ferable to the abject terms of furrender-
ing at difcretion; and they formed the
defperate refolution of fetting fire to the
town, and forcing their way in the con-
fufion through the Englifh lines (f).
This wild enterprize was prevented by
the more liberal proceedings of a fecond
conference, wherein Chichelé, and the

(f) Monftrelet, chap. 202.

commiffioners

commiffioners joined with him for 'that purpofe, having opened a negotiation with the fix deputies from Rouen, it was finally agreed *(g)* that the citizens fhould pay 365,000 crowns of gold, and fwear allegiance to the Englifh fovereign : and that the garrifon fhould take an oath not to appear in arms againft him for the fpace of one year. Thefe preliminaries being adjufted, the royal army entered the city in triumph January 19 *(h)*.

1419.

RELIEVED from the long miferies of a defolating fiege, even the conquered muft have partaken in the exultation of the victors. Their joy was repreffed for a fhort interval by the intrufion of one fanguinary act : from the general pardon

(g) Monftrelet, chap. 202.   *(h)* Ibid.

Henry's

Henry's indignation reserved a single
victim. Alain Blanchard, whose patrio-
tic virtue had protracted the glorious resistance of his fellow citizens, closed a
life, deserving of a far different fate, under
the hands of the executioner *(i)*.

CHICHELE' continued in France till
the latter end of the summer *(k)*: the
care of his province then called him
home. On his arrival he issued letters
mandatory to his suffragans, to order public prayers throughout their several diocefes for the king's safety. He foon
after summoned a convocation, in which,
on his representation of the necessity of
fresh supplies, the clergy granted half a
tenth; with the addition of six shillings
and eight pence to be assessed upon every

(i) Monstrelet, 202.
(k) Act. Pub. tom. iv. part 2d. p. 124.

F　　　　　　perfon

perſon poſſeſſed of a chapel or chauntry,
or who enjoyed a regular ſtipend for the
ſervice of a church; under a formal
proteſt, that this addition ſhould not be
drawn into a precedent. The other bu-
ſineſs of the meeting was the cenſure of
a prieſt accuſed of witchcraft, and the re-
prehenſion of ſome diſciples of Wickliffe *(l)*, who on their recantation were
1420. diſmiſſed with impunity. In the May
following he devolved the government
of his dioceſe on his vicar general, and
repaired to Troyes, to congratulate his
ſovereign in perſon on the concluſion of
a peace with France, and a marriage with

(l) The diſciples of Wickliffe were generally dif-
tinguiſhed by the appellation of Lollards, a name
borrowed from a ſect in the low countries, and derived
to them from the cuſtom of ſinging a requiem to the
ſouls of the deceaſed; the German word *loller* ſignify-
ing to *lull* or *ſooth*.

Moſheim Ecclef. Hiſt. vol. i. p. 744.

Catharine;

Catharine *(m)*; two events that were happily accomplished at this time, and which gave Henry the title of Regent of France with the authority of king. From Troyes Chichelé attended Henry to the sieges of Montereau and Melun. The latter of these places was defended by the Dauphin's party for more than four months, and every post disputed with the most unrelaxing obstinacy. The presence of the king and queen of France gave the camp, amidst all the hurry and confusion incident to such a scene, more splendor and festivity than any other in Henry's wars. They held their court in a pavilion removed beyond the reach

---

(m) The marriage was performed by the archbishop of Sens, whom Henry, after the capture of that city, reinstated in his see with these words, " Vous " m'avez epousé et baillé une femme, je vous rends " la votre." Villaret, tom. vii. p. 272.

of

of the enemy's cannon; the day was uſhered in and concluded with the cheerful harmony of ten horns from the Engliſh band, and the charms of muſic were heightened by the luſtre of ſome of the brighteſt beauties in the kingdom (*n*). Catharine, the new-married queen, attended by the duchefs of Clarence and a train of Engliſh ladies, reſided at Corbueïl, not far diſtant from Melun. Hither the king often retired, to forget the horrors of war in the ſociety of a young and beautiful bride (*o*). During the whole courſe of this campaign Chichelé was preſent, and contributed as uſual to temper the ferocity of military manners, and the licentiouſneſs of a camp, by the mild ſuggeſtions

(*n*) Monſtrelet, chap. 228. tom. i.
(*o*) Ibid.

of

of humanity, and the influence of religious example.

From Melun he attended the court to Paris, and revisited England in November. The king and queen arrived there early in the next year, and were received by their subjects with every attestation of joy and loyalty. Prayers were offered up by Chichelé's injunction four days successively, and the satisfaction of the people was consummated in the coronation of their royal mistress; a ceremony that was performed by the hands of the archbishop.

1421.

While the populace expressed their exultation in shouts and public shews, the parliament gave a more substantial proof of their affection, in a liberal grant for the maintenance of the war against

F 3

the

the dauphin's party. The clergy were at the fame time convened by Chichelé, and granted the crown a tenth; on condition that the poffeffions of the church fhould continue to be exempted from the burthen of purveyance, and that eccle-fiaftics fhould be permitted to give bail in all crimes, except open theft and murder. Another provifion *(p)* made in this fynod feems to betray a con-fcioufnefs in the facred body of frailties which the reftraints of the facerdotal character were perhaps more calculated to aggravate than control; unlefs we fuppofe them to have guarded againft an injury they were never likely to provoke.

The fees of inftitution and induction were by a new regulation now mode-

(p) Ut ii qui facerdotes caftrarent feloniæ crimine tenerentur. A. Duck.

rated,

rated, and bishops and archdeacons forbidden to take more for their respective trouble than twelve shillings. It was decreed likewise, that ordination should in future be conferred without any gratuity or reward.

THE Pope's collector met with little attention from this synod in an application he made for a grant to his holiness; it appearing to the whole assembly, that the yearly tenths, and other regular payments to the court of Rome, were as much as the necessities of the kingdom would allow.

CHICHELE' having dissolved the assembly turned his thoughts to the preservation of his jurisdiction in France; and, to the intent that he might reconcile the two churches, he recalled the judges

whom

whom he had set over the diocefes fubject to England, and left the care of them
to their bifhops, and the ordinary magif-
trates of the feveral diftricts in which
they were fituated.

THE news of Clarence's death, who
had fallen in a fkirmifh with the dauphin's troops near Baugé in the province of Anjou, threw an univerfal damp
upon the public joy. He was a great
and deferved favourite of the nation, and
to the moft romantic valour added a re-
finement of manners, not common in
the politeft courts of Europe *(q)*. The
influence of fo amiable a character was
not confined to the narrow circle of
friends, he is faid to have died lamented
even by the enemy *(r)*. This unfortu-

(q) (r) Montfaucon. Monum. de la Monarch.
Franc. p. 177.

nate

nate event haſtened the king's journey
into France *(s)*; and during his abſence
the queen was delivered at Windſor of a
prince, who ſucceeded his father by the
title of Henry VI. He was baptized by
Chichelé early in December, and, when
he afterwards came to the throne, received the crown from the hands of the
ſame prelate.

(s) In this laſt viſit of Henry to the French dominions he diſplayed a very engaging inſtance of gene-
roſity. Sir Oliver Manny, an old knight who had
broken his parole, was taken priſoner and ſent to the
king then at Meaux. The law of arms puniſhed this
breach of honour with death ; royal clemency was
ſatisfied with a milder penalty. " Fair father," ſaid
Henry, " you have ſworn unto us never to bear arms
" againſt us or our ſubjects, you are an ancient
" knight, and ſhould have kept your faith, which ye
" have untruly and unhoneſtly violated ; yet, though
" by the law of arms we might, we will not put you
" to death ; we will ſend you to *England to learn the*
" *language of that country.*"
Hollingſhed, vol. ii. p. 581.

In

In the Auguſt of 1422 the archbiſhop convoked a general meeting of the
clergy, to make choice of proper deputies
to attend the council of Conſtance,
which, in purſuance of a plan for renew-
ing it every fifth year, was to be convened this autumn at Pavia. This
ſcheme was however fruſtrated; the
council being firſt removed to Sienna on
account of the plague, and there diſſolv-
ed by the pope. One White was in the
ſame ſynod cenſured for having preached
without a licence, and Henry Webb ſen-
tenced to be thrice publicly whipped
for performing the ſacred office before he
was in holy orders. A delinquent of a
more heinous ſort was William Taylor:
he had maintained that God alone was
to be worſhipped, and that all devotion
to ſaints or images was idolatry. Chichelé

chelé referred the confideration of his offence to the four orders of mendicant fryars, who, having found that his opi- nions were not conformable either to the fcriptures or the doctrines of the fathers, pronounced him guilty of he- refy. Lyndewode, dean of the court of arches, the official of Canterbury, and other profeffors of the civil and canon laws, declared, that by thofe laws he was on conviction to be delivered over to the fecular arm.

THIS fynod was fcarcely brought to a conclufion, when intelligence of the king's death fpread a general confterna- tion throughout the kingdom. He died at Bois de Vincennes, Monday the laft day of Auguft. His remains were with great funeral pomp tranfported to Eng- land, and depofited with thofe of his an- ceftors.

ceftors. His queen attended the melancholy proceffion at a fmall diftance *(t)*, and in this affectionate and forrowful act of conjugal duty took a laft farewell of her native country and earlieft connections.

From Henry Vth's death we may date the decline of England's fhort-lived power in France. The ftately fabric erected by his active prowefs gradually mouldered away under the feeble and unfettled adminiftration of his unfortunate heir.

To every lover of his country the condition of the French dominions muft have appeared truly deplorable. The inceffant ravages of feven years of war had reduced a great part of that realm to the

(*t*) Stowe, p. 363.

moft

most ruinous state : exclusive of some villages, which were rather military posts than the peaceful habitations of peasants, from the banks of the Loire to the sea coast all was desert. Agriculture, the most necessary of human inventions, suffered in the common wreck of every useful art : the few labourers who remained to till the soil retired from fields infested by nightly marauders at the sound of the evening bell, a warning that even the cattle instinctively obeyed *(u)*. To add to the horror, the wolves were so multiplied that officers were appointed expressly for the destruction of them; and they were entitled to levy a contribution on every family within two leagues of the spot on which a wolf was

(u) Meyer, quoted by Gollut in his Memoirs of the House of Burgundy, pag. 717.

killed

killed *(x)*; an extent that implies a great want of population.

ANY attempt to draw the character of a prince fo well known as Henry V. might in this place be confidered as impertinent. One of the leading features in it feems to have been inflexible firmnefs; of which Hollingfhed may be thought, perhaps, to have given a whimfical example, when he tells us, " that " he was never feen to turn his nofe " from an evil favour, nor clofe his eyes " from fmoke or duft."

(x) Act. Pub. tom. iv. part 3d. p. 158.

SECTION

SECTION V.

BY the late king's appointment the goverment of England devolved upon Humphry duke of Glocefter *(a)*, who fummoned without delay a meeting of Parliament at Weftminfter. Chichelé opened to the affembly the reafons of their being called together; and, after paying a grateful tribute of praife to the memory of his deceafed fovereign, rifked fome fanguine prefages of the profperous reign of his infant heir: intimating, in the quaint and pedantic eloquence of

(a) His falary as protector was fixed by parliament, in 1423, at eight thoufand marks a year.

Act. Pub. tom. iv. part 4th. p. 86.

3

that

1422.

that æra, " that whereby God had made " all things in fix days, fo he would " accomplifh all the good beginnings of " the famous fifth Henry in the fixth " Henry his fon *(b)* ;" a declaration that certainly was not dictated by the fpirit of prophecy. On the diffolution of this parliament Chichelé retired to his diocefe, and, difengaged from politi-cal occupations, dedicated his whole time

1423.

to the duties of his province. In 1423 he made a progrefs through the diocefes of Chichefter and Salifbury. The fee of Lincoln was referved for the follow-

1424.

ing year. A diligent inquiry into the morals and religion of the inhabitants, and a careful reform of feveral abufes that through indolence or inattention had eluded the notice of his predeceffors,

(b) Cotton's Abridgment, pag. 560.

marked

marked the courfe of the archbifhop's paftoral journies. The lively impreffion of early pleafures is hardly ever oblite-rated by the bufieft fcenes of a maturer age. The opportunity offered to Chi-chelé, in this laft vifitation, of again be-holding a fpot familiar to him in his youth, was not neglected, and the fight of Higham-ferrers revived within him all his former partialities. His munifi-cence there will find a place more pro-perly in the fequel of thefe fheets.

FROM this furvey his attention was within a fhort time called to another fy-nod, in which the bifhops of Winchefter and Bath exerted all their powers of elo-cution to obtain a grant for the fervice of the war. But, whether the refources of the clergy were exhaufted by the li-beral fupplies already granted, or all con-

G   fidence

fidence of victory was buried in the grave with Henry the Vth. this unpromising point was laboured in vain. William Lyndewode, who was deputed by the fynod to deliver their fentiments, argued, that the poffeffions had been fo much im-poverifhed by repeated exactions, that the refidue was inadequate to the decent fupport of the members in general, while the fmaller benefices were fo reduced by continual drains as to be fcarce worth acceptance *(c)*. The fynod was pro-

rogued to February in the enfuing year, when Chichelé and the bifhop of Win-chefter urged the old topic of a fubfidy

(c) In the current year Chichelé was relieved by order of council from the charge of Robert Girefme, a French prifoner committed to his cuftody by the late king. This practice of intrufting prifoners of note to private cuftody was not uncommon.

Act. Pub. tom. iv. part 4. pag. 105.

with

with great warmth : but, as the interefts of the ecclefiaftical body at large could be preferved only by a ftrict correfpondence between the conftituent parts, the upper houfe of convocation would engage in no meafures which were not approved by the delegates of the lower order, and thefe remained inexorable.

Chichele', defpairing from the temper of this affembly of any fuccefs, appointed a frefh fynod to be convened in May; yet fo inconfiderable was the change of fentiments wrought by this expedient, that neither entreaties nor menaces could prevail on the reprefentatives of the clergy to contribute more to the affiftance of government than half a tenth. The fame co-operation could not fail of accompanying the proceedings of the fynod, when they were

G 2   directed

directed solely to the maintenance of religion and the censure of heresy. Two secular priests, Hoke and Drayton, were convicted of holding heretical opinions; but, as in cases of this nature the readiest path to pardon was abjuration, the criminals were absolved on formally renouncing their errors at St. Paul's crofs. William Ruffel, a friar minorite, to the crime of deviating from the established doctrines of the church added an attack upon its privileges; he had not only taught publicly, that a free intercourse of the sexes was not incompatible with the purity of a monastic life, but had afferted from the pulpit that tithes were not of divine inftitution. He escaped immediate punifhment by abfconding. Meantime this deviation from established tenets drew upon him the indignation of the two univerfities of Oxford and Cambridge;

and

and the former paffed a decree, prohibiting the prefentation of any perfon to an
academical degree, who had not folemnly
declared his abhorrence of Ruffel's opinions (d). To obviate any dangerous
impreffion upon the minds of the illite-
rate from thefe novel doctrines, Chichelé
commanded the Francifcans, an order
of friars who enjoyed the greateft popularity as preachers, to inculcate the divine right of the church to tithes in their
conftant difcourfes. The office of pro-
locutor or fpeaker of the lower houfe of
convocation was, for the firft time, regularly fettled by this fynod; and, at the
archbifhop's recommendation, that office was given to William Lyndewode,
a man every way qualified for the difcharge of it. In the fame year Lynde-

(d) A. Wood. Hift. Univ. Oxon. L. i. p. 210.

wode

S ᴇ ᴄ ᴛ,
V.

1426.

wode was deputed by Chichelé to vifit
the colleges in Oxford fubject to his ju-
rifdiction, an undertaking in which he
was affifted by Thomas Bronns. They began their vifitation with Merton college,
and, having made feveral ordinances for
the government of that fociety, extended
their furvey to the whole univerfity except queen's and new college *(e)*.

WHILST the clergy had been unwill-
ingly granting their quota in convocation, the king, then under three years of
age, took his feat in the great affembly
of the nation. The royal child had been
brought by eafy journies from Windfor.
The firft night he refted at Stanes ; on
the fecond he reached Kingfton ; the
third he paffed at his manor of Kenning-

(ı) A. Wood. L. ı. p. 217.

ton ;

ton; and on the fourth entered Weſtminſter ſitting in the queen's lap; who
from an open carriage held out their infant ſovereign to the eager gaze of his
loyal ſubjects (f).

Aɴ unhappy difference between the
protector and the biſhop of Wincheſter
called aloud at this ſeaſon for the friendly
interpoſition of ſome powerful mediator.
The diſſenſion of theſe noble adverſaries
had attained to ſuch a height, that the general peace and welfare of the metropolis
was in the moſt imminent danger. The
ſhops were ſhut, all traffick obſtructed, and
the citizens occupied in keeping watch
and ward, to prevent the miſchiefs which
the hoſtile appearance of the partizans
in this alarming quarrel hourly threat-

(f) Fabian's Chron. fol. 410.

G 4 ned.

ned. Neither the benevolence of his heart, nor the dignity of his ftation, would fuffer Chichelé to remain an indifferent fpectator of an occurrence pregnant with fuch difaftrous confequences. With the duke of Coimbra prince of Portugal, then on a vifit to the Englifh court, he rode eight times in one day between the two competitors, to bring their difpute to an accommodation. This timely interference reftrained the violence of their animofity, but did not extinguifh their fecret refentments. In a letter to the duke of Bedford the bifhop of Winchefter expreffed himfelf in terms that by no means implied a fincere reconciliation. " Hafte you hither" (fays the bifhop) " for by my truth, if you " tarry, we fhall put this land in adven- " ture with a field, fuch a brother have " you

" you here *(g)*." Bedford thought it
too urgent a bufinefs to admit of any delay, and haftening over fummoned a
parliament at Leicefter. Articles were
here exhibited by Glocefter againft the
bifhop, and referred to the arbitration of
Chichelé and a committee of temporal
and fpiritual peers; who, upon a candid
and deliberate difcuffion of them, judged
that the duke and bifhop fhould, after
reciprocal conceffions in a form of words
prefcribed to them for that purpofe, take
each other by the hand, and exchange
forgivenefs in prefence of the king and
parliament *(h)*. We need not look for
the origin of this difagreement in any
particular infult; perfonal provocations,
however trivial, foon inflame a mifunder-
ftanding occafioned by rivalfhip. The

(g) Hollingfhed, vol. ii. p. 591.
(h) Ibid. p. 595.

haughty

haughty prelate of Winchefter could ill brook the fuperior power of a youthful protector; and Glocefter was not inclined by any fhew of deference to gratify the pride or conciliate the friendfhip of an overbearing churchman. The effects of an imprudent attachment had recently given too folid a plea for complaints againft the protector, who had weakened the few forces left for the defence of the kingdom by a confiderable levy of men for the profecution of his wife's claims in the Netherlands; and eftranged from the intereft of the Englifh government the duke of Burgundy, its moft powerful ally. But while we condemn the *Protector* for a marriage highly unjuftifiable in a political light, we fhould temper the feverity of our cenfures by a recollection of the temptations that folicited *Glocefter* to this connection.

I   Jaqueline

Jaqueline of Hainault, the object of his paffion, poffeffed attractions fufficient to have inflamed a bofom lefs fufceptible of love and ambition than that of this prince. The only daughter and heirefs of William duke of Bavaria, fhe was born to the rich reverfion of the provinces of Hainault, Holland, and Zealand. With her perfon a joint intereft in all thefe hereditary poffeffions was firft conferred upon a fon of France. His death foon left her at liberty to beftow them elfewhere. Contiguous dominions and the requeft of a dying parent, rather than any perfonal affection, induced her to make choice of the duke of Brabant for her fecond hufband. Difference of age and fentiments, and a wide difproportion in their abilities, combined to produce a coolnefs which fhortly terminated in feparation. He was of tender years, of a

fickly

fickly conftitution, and a flow and dull intellect; indolent and unimpaffioned in private life, and blindly abandoned to the guidance of a worthlefs fet of favourites in his public capacity. Jaqueline was in every refpect the reverfe : in the bloom of health and full vigour of age, fhe poffeffed an underftanding fuperior to that of any contemporary of her fex. Her perfonal charms did not difparage the endowments of her mind; a beautiful and expreffive countenance, an elegant fhape and winning manners, gave a commanding influence to the dictates of a high fpirit and ftrong paffions (i). Having under pretext of their nearnefs in blood quitted the fociety of her hufband, fhe fled into England, and was received in a manner fuitable to her rank

(i) Henæus Annal. of Brabant, pag. 399, 400, 401, 402.

and

and the dignity of that crown. She was married in the courfe of a few months to the duke of Glocefter, and in 1423 accompanied him into Hainault. On his return fhe was left at Mons to the protection of the inhabitants, who had fworn to defend the perfon of their miftrefs at all hazards. Their allegiance was not proof againft the menaces of the duke of Burgundy, to whom the garrifon foon furrendered her, having received no reinforcement from England. She had fent repeated intelligence of her calamitous fituation to Glocefter, and omitted in her letters no confideration that could urge him to come to her relief: fhe calls upon him, by the tender and endearing addrefs of lord and father, to fuccour the diftrefs of a forrowful and beloved child, whofe only confolation is that fhe fuffers on his account; fhe af-

6

fures

SECT.
V.

fures him that to do his pleafure has been, and ever fhall be, her chief happinefs, and that fhe is ready to meet death for his fake *(k)*. Language like this muft have been either the refult of warm and fincere affection, or of womanifh fears; her fubfequent conduct will fcarcely permit us to adopt the latter fufpicion. After a fhort confinement at Ghent fhe made her efcape in man's clothes, and mounting a horfe in this difguife did not alight till fhe reached Antwerp. Here fhe refumed the habit of her fex, and purfued her journey to Holland. The duke of Burgundy followed her with a formidable power. Undaunted fhe appeared at the head of her troops, led them in perfon to the fiege of Haerlem, and underwent all the fatigues of a fevere

(k) Monftrelet, vol. ii. fol. 24.

campaign,

campaign, with a refolution that amply
compenfated for the abfence of mafcu-
line ftrength and a more robuft frame.
Glocefter's defertion of her, and the
death of the duke of Brabant, releafed
her at once from all engagements; and
fhe furvived about ten years, in peace and
fecurity, a treaty, by which fhe inftitu-
ted her coufin the duke of Burgundy
heir to all her poffeffions *(l)*.

To return to a fubject from which
I have been drawn into an unwarrantable digreffion *. Chichelé quitted
the

(l) Haræus Ann. Brab. as above.

* In apology for this digreffion I have nothing to
offer but the popularity of Jaqueline's character,
whofe imprifonment not only drew a bold remonftrance from " a large body of females of good ac-
" count and well apparelled," fays Stowe, but was
taken up in a high ftrain by the commons, who peti-
tioned

the parliament at Leicefter in May, and repairing to London affembled a fynod there. The fame parcimonious maxims that regulated the proceedings of the laft meeting ftill prevailed, and the eccle-fiaftics paid with reluctance what they had granted fparingly *(m)*.

tioned for her relief; and, to give the greater weight to their petition, tacked it to the grant of a fubfidy.

Parl. Hift. vol. ii. p. 212, 213.

(m) It was in this year that Chichelé received by an act of council a falary of 300 marks a year for his attendance as one of that body. The bifhop of Win-chefter had the fame appointment, and inferior members, both fpiritual and temporal, ftipends proportionate to their rank. Act. Pub. tom. iv. part 4. p. 122.

SECTION.

SECTION VI.

MARTIN the fifth, one of the fturdieft pontiffs that ever filled the papal chair, had long regarded with a jealous eye thofe falutary barriers againft the encroachments of the court of Rome, the ftatutes of provifors and præmunire. The reftrictions which thefe acts laid him under grew every day more irkfome to him, and he had particularly exerted himfelf in the courfe of the laft year to obtain a repeal of them. His remonftrances, however preffing, were ineffectual; and, as he conceived his defigns to have mifcarried from Chichelé's difaffection to the caufe, his refentments

H   were

were more immediately levelled at him. The correspondence which this variance introduced between the pope and the archbishop throws no inconsiderable light on the character of them both : and though it was productive of much severe treatment of Chichelé, the honourable testimony borne to his integrity and abilities by the nation in general was a recompence equivalent to any mortification he could suffer in the progress of this affair. From the imperfect records that have reached us relative to this transaction it appears, that Martin's intention of suspending the legatine power *(a)*, hi-

(*a*) This suspension of the legatine power, for which Martin had actually issued a bull, I conjecture to have been the hardship which Chichelé complains of in the course of his controversy, as never having been attempted from the first foundation of the see.

Wilkins's Concil. tom. iii. pag. 474, 484.

therto

therto annexed to the metropolitan fee, had been intimated to Chichelé fo early as the commencement of the prefent year. Upon this information he on the twenty-fecond of March made a formal appeal to the firft general council that fhould be affembled, from all decifions which Martin or his fucceffors might make prejudicial to his rights as primate. On the twenty-feventh of the fame month the archbifhop, then in his palace at Canterbury, was prefented, by the hands of John de Obizis, the pope's nun‑ tio, with certain bulls, the contents of which he was yet a ftranger to, when the lieutenant of Dover caftle brought him orders to fend any packets he had re‑ ceived from Rome immediately to the protector. This verbal injunction was foon followed by a writ, commanding him, on the reception of any future bulls

or

SECT.
VI.

or public letters from the pope, to tranf-
mit them unopened to the council.

THOUGH thefe meafures are a proof
that Chichelé wanted neither fpirit to af-
fert the privileges of the Englifh church,
nor the fupport of his fovereign in the
maintenance of them, he neverthelefs
felt himfelf by no means eafy in his fituation.. Papal cenfures were ftill formidable, and the belief of the fundamen-
tal doctrines of the catholic religion was
fo clofely interwoven in vulgar minds
with a firm perfuafion of the fupreme
minifter's infallibility, that no prudent
friend to the former would have endeavoured to degrade or weaken the authority of the latter.- The archbifhop faw
the full force of this confideration, and,
unwilling to afford the flighteft fhadow
of encouragement to the unorthodox no-

tions

tions which had of late been promul-
gated by the lollard sectaries, instead of
open resistance to the pontiff's will, tried
the gentler method of soothing intreaties
and humble reprefentation. In a letter
dated the tenth of March he had endeavoured to blunt the edge of Martin's refentment by the most fubmiffive profeffions of duty. By the fame opportunity
he addreffed an epistle to feveral cardinals, to beg their interceffion. The pope
in anfwer to thefe applications informs
him, that an immediate compliance
with his request, to have the execrable
statutes in question repealed, would be
the most convincing argument he could
employ to prove the fincerity of his
profeffions. He adds, that the archbifhop had been reported to him to have
fpoken very irreverently of his zeal in
this holy caufe, as arifing from motives
of covetoufnefs and "a defire of enrich-

H 3   " ing

" ing himself at the expence of the na-
" tion;" and cautions him not to bestow
that reproach on others, which would
appear upon reflection more suitable to
his own conduct. Chichelé, in return,
complains of the misreprefentations he
labours under at his holiness's court
from the calumny of his enemies, and
the impossibility, from age and infirmities,
of his exculpating himself in person; he
alludes likewise to fome steps that were
in contemplation against the rights of
the fee of Canterbury, never before attempted, at least as he collects from
report: fince, as he was under a prohi-
bition from opening his holiness's public
difpatches, he could not gain more certain knowledge of his intentions.

CHICHELE' was not thus expofed to the
perfecution of the apoftolic fee without
interefting the nation in his caufe. The
ecclefiaftics

ecclefiaftics were the firft who ftood forth in his defence: a very dutiful letter was addreffed to Martin, fubfcribed by fixteen bifhops, in which they affure him that the archbifhop had been grofsly flandered; that he was, contrary to the infinuations of his enemies, confidered by the bulk of the nation as a faithful and prudent fteward; while that part of it which was more immediately connected with him by profeffion, which had more opportunities, and more interefted motives jealoufly to watch his conduct, had ever looked up to him as a father. The univerfity of Oxford were not lefs warm in their vidication of him. They tell the pope, " that Chichelé ftood in the fanctuary of God as a firm wall that herefy could not fhake nor fimony undermine; that he was the darling of the people, and the fofter-parent of the clergy."

H 4

clergy." To thefe flattering teftimonies was added that of feveral temporal lords, who, after exculpating him on the general heads of accufation, to obviate the pope's imputation of covetoufnefs, particularize his fingular liberality in having conftantly reftored the whole of the fpiritualities which he might, during the vacancy of the bifhoprics within his province, juftly have in part detained. They further mention, that in cafes of poverty he frequently affifted from his own purfe fuch-as were appointed to benefices by papal provifion. Before thefe addreffes arrived at the court of Rome, Martin had received Chichelé's excufes by the hand of a faithful agent; whofe reprefentations feem, by the fofter fpirit of the pope's anfwer, to have allayed in great meafure the afperity of his refentment. His refolution however was

immutably

immutably fixed; and in purfuance of
it he in October wrote both to the king
and parliament, in a very dictatorial ftyle,
to procure the repeal of the ftatutes of
provifions and præmunire in the next
feffion. Chichelé received an admoni-
tion to the fame purport. But as no immediate effect was produced by thefe
applications, Martin refumed his autho-
ritative tone both to the king and the
archbifhop: " Read (fays he to the latter)
" read that royal ftatute, (if an act which
" fubverts the laws of God and the
" church deferves fuch a title) and judge,
" venerable brother, you who are a
" chriftian and catholic bifhop, if the
" difciples of chriftianity can confcien-
" tioufly obferve it : a ftatute by which
" the king difpofes of ecclefiaftical pre-
" ferments as abfolutely as if Chrift had
" ordained him his vicar, and affumes
" the

" the fupremacy in fpiritual matters " with as high a hand as if the keys of " St. Peter had been delivered into his " cuftody." He concludes this angry epiftle with directions to Chichelé, under pain of excommunication, to ufe all his influence with the parliament for the abrogation of thefe deteftable acts : and doubting the efficacy of arguments founded upon fo fhallow a bafis, againft the good fenfe of the reprefentatives of the people, he further commands him to alarm the confciences of the lower ranks on this nice queftion, by an injunction to the inferior clergy to preach upon it. At the fame time, to fhow the archbifhop how little confidence was repofed in him, he is commanded to fend to Rome a full account of his progrefs attefted by at leaft two credible witneffes : a flight of a fimilar nature to that paffed

6   on

on him in a letter addreſſed jointly to
the two archbiſhops, wherein Martin
with a puerile ſpleen gives the ſee of
York the precedence. In conſequence
of the laſt thundering epiſtle Chichelé,
accompanied by the archbiſhop of York,
and ſeveral of their ſuffragans, attended
the commons in the refectory of the ab-
bey of Weſtminſter, their uſual place of
aſſembling; and having declared previ-
ouſly, that he and his brethren did not
mean to offer any thing either in prejudice of the king's prerogative or the
common weal, he entered into a deſcription of the civil and eccleſiaſtical juriſ-
diction, pointed out the barrier between
the church and ſtate, and drew a lively
picture of the deſtructive conſequences
that would reſult from the kingdom
being laid under an interdict. He at
length withdrew, but not till he had
preſſed

preſſed the critical temper of affairs with an earneſtneſs which brought tears into his eyes.

THE commons did not adopt the arch-biſhop's ſentiments with reſpect to the papal ſee : uninfluenced by his argu-ments, they were not however inſenſible to the difficulties of his ſituation ; nor did they conclude the ſeſſion before they had preſented a petition to the king, praying his mediation with the pope in Chichelé's behalf *(b)* : and here this troubleſome and vexatious diſpute fell to the ground *(c)* *.

THAT

(b) Rolls of Parl. vol. iv. p. 322.

(c) Wilkins's Concil. vol. iii. from p. 471 to 487.

* The only authentic materials to be found rela-tive to this tranſaction are I believe preſerved in Wil-kins's Concilia : but, as theſe materials are not al-ways

THAT thefe proceedings were conducted by Martin with fo little delicacy
towards the archbifhop, may be attributed to the fteady and early oppofition
that prelate had fhewn to papal claims,
whenever he thought them incompatible
with the privileges of the church of
England *(d)*.

AMONGST many inftances of this nature, one has obtained particular notice:
while the late king was abfent from his

ways either regularly arranged or accurately dated, I
have, where I thought myfelf warranted by the con-
text, by the inconfiftency of the dates as there given,
and by a comparifon of them with the rolls of parliament and other undoubted records, ventured, not
without diffidence, to vary from them. As Duck
had not entered into this part of Chichelé's hiftory, a
full and clear detail of it became more neceffary, and
the probability of fucceeding more remote.

(d) Walfingham's Hypodygma Neuftriæ, p. 579.

dominions

dominions in the profecution of the French war, the Roman pontiff was bufily employed in the execution of a defign he then entertained, of appointing Beaufort bifhop of Winchefter a cardinal, and legate *a latere* for England during life. This fcheme was defeated by Chichelé's vigilance, who reprefented *(e)* the impropriety of fuch an appointment fo effectually to Henry, that he declared he would rather fee his uncle Beaufort invefted with his crown than with a cardinal's hat. This honour he had fince obtained on his arrival at Calais with the duke of Bedford in the courfe of the laft year. He was at this time returned into England with legatine authority. But as the king's proctor protefted againft the entrance of a legate

(e) See Letter in Appendix N° II.

into

into the realm of England without the sovereign's permiſſion, the cardinal-biſhop was obliged to declare before the lords of parliament, that he would attempt nothing prejudicial to the rights of the crown, and exerciſe no branch of his office till he had obtained the royal leave. The motive which principally induced the pope to make Beaufort a cardinal at this juncture was, that in the character of legate he might preach up a cruſade againſt the Huſſites, an obſtinate ſect of heretics in Bohemia which gave the court of Rome much trouble; and it was with this view he now viſited England.

To forward the purpoſes of this holy miſſion Chichelé was ordered to injoin public prayers and proceſſions for the converſion of theſe deluded heretics: and,

that

that no encouragement might be wanting to good catholics in this religious
undertaking, Martin offered indulgences
(f) for a hundred days to all such as de-
voutly rehearſed the ſeven penitential
pſalms, or twenty-five pater-noſters and
ave-marias, for the accompliſhment of the
pious work. In conformity to the pope's
bull fit perſons were appointed alſo by
the archbiſhop, to publiſh this cruſade,
and to grant abſolution to ſuch as were
willing to engage in the holy warfare.
In the month of July Chichelé convok-

(f) In another bull Martin holds out ſtill more
alluring terms of invitation to the volunteers in this
pious cauſe. Seven years remiſſion of penance to all
who contributed in the proportion of the thouſandth
penny of their property; and an unlimited forgive-
neſs of paſt enormities of every ſpecies to ſuch as
ſerved half a year in perſon, or found a ſoldier in this
cruſade.—— Faſciculus, publiſhed from Regiſter of
Canterbury by E. Brown.

ed

ed à fynod at St. Paul's cathedral. The
bufinefs of thefe affemblies was limited
to few points, and the relation admits of
little variety. Amongft feveral perfons
accufed of herefy before this tribunal, Catharine Dertford feems to have excited
very unreafonable apprehenfions. Being
queftioned relative to fome abftrufe doctrines of the church, fhe with great fimplicity confeffed, that her information in
religious matters was confined to the
knowledge of the creed and the ten
commandments. Ralph Mungyn, a fecular prieft, who wanted thofe pleas for
compaffion which her inexperience and
her fex gave this female, had neverthelefs little room for complaint either of
the perfecuting fpirit or the harfh pro-
ceeding of his judge. Chichelé repeatedly exhorted him with parental tender-
nefs to renounce his errors, and repeatedly

adjourned

adjourned the fentence of condemnation.
Finding all argument ineffectual, he at
length pronounced on him the doom of
perpetual imprifonment, ftill referving a
power of mitigating this punifhment, if
time and reflection fhould bring the
unhappy object of it to a fenfe of his de-
linquency *(g)*. The fynod was continued with fhort intermiffions to December, and a fubfidy of half a tenth granted

to the crown: in the enfuing October
the further grant of a tenth and a half
was levied in convocation to the fame
ufe. By this well-timed liberality the
clergy obtained a privilege, which hitherto had been wanting, to give their
meeting freedom and fecurity: an act
was on their petition paffed, providing
that their delegates, during the fitting of

(g) Wilkins's Concil. vol. iii. p. 502.

convocation,

convocation, fhould enjoy exemption from
arrefts, and every other immunity poffeffed by the members of the lower houfe
of parliament.   Under thefe promifing
appearances the convocation was diffolv-
ed; and Conzo, the pope's nuntio, who
had long folicited a tenth, faw its diffolution without having been able to procure one favourable hearing.   This neglect furnifhed frefh matter for Martin's
indignation againft Chichelé, whom he
confidered as one of the chief obftructors
of his agent's fuccefs.   The archbifhop,
to remove the wrong impreffions the
pope had received, wrote a very refpectful
apology for his conduct, in which he
particularly alleges, that he had purpof-
edly protracted the fynod to October, that
no impediment to the execution of his
holinefs's defires might lie in him *(b)*.

(b) See letter in Appendix N° 2.

I 2   In

Iɴ fourteen hundred and thirty Chi-chelé summoned another assembly of his clergy. Ecclesiastical censures formed, as usual, the bulk of the business transacted in this meeting. The enforcement of spiritual decrees by temporal penalties was no uncommon occurrence: but in one instance spiritual terrors were made subsidiary to civil justice. The fraudulent practice of using a false weight, which had long prevailed amongst unfair traders notwithstanding the endeavours of the civil magistrate, drew the notice of this synod; and Chichelé published a formal sentence of excommunication against all who in future should dare to use it.

Cᴀʀᴅɪɴᴀʟ Bᴇᴀᴜꜰᴏʀᴛ, who had embarked with levies for the Bohemian crusade in July, did not reach Bohemia till the

the next year, having ſtipulated to aſſiſt the duke of Bedford with his forces for the term of ſix months: nor does it appear that he conducted himſelf perfectly to the pope's ſatisfaction on his arrival; ſince he was ſoon ſuperſeded, and return-ed again to England. The appointment of cardinal Julian of Saint Angelo legate was one of the laſt acts of that reſtleſs pontiff Martin the fifth. He died in February fourteen hundred and thirty- 1431. one, and by his death reſtored to Chi-chelé a proſpect of that repoſe and tran-quillity which his advanced age and growing infirmities ſo much required.

SECTION

SECTION VII.

AT the opening of this year Chichelé was appointed to act as commiffioner, for raifing money to defray the expences of the king's journey to France. This vifit Henry undertook at the preffing folicitation of the duke of Bedford, who faw, in defiance of his moft vigorous exertions, the Englifh intereft declining in that country with rapid paces. Among many incidents which had confpired to produce a change in the face of affairs, the late fingular fucceffes of the Maid of Orleans were certainly not the leaft important. Her extraordinary

traordinary miſſion, and the reſt of thoſe

marvellous forgeries which formed the texture of her myſterious ſtory, whether they are to be conſidered as the dreams of a viſionary enthuſiaſt, or the bold fictions of an enlightened politician, were well calculated to inſpire her countrymen with confidence, and give new vigour to their arms : and however ill founded the terror of her name may have been, it ſtruck ſo univerſal an awe into the Engliſh ſoldiers, that they deſerted in large bodies *(a)*. No leſs than three pro-

I 4   clamations

(a) The effects of Joan's termagant ſpirit were not, if we may believe a contemporary writer, reſtrained to her enemies. She had been a very ſhort time in poſſeſſion of the ſword which ſhe boaſted to have been diſcovered to her by divine revelation, when ſhe broke it upon two or three looſe followers of the camp ; much to her ſovereign's diſſatisfaction, who chidingly told her, that ſhe ſhould rather have taken a good *ſtick* to them. " Il y avoit" (ſays this author)

SECT.
VII.

1431.

clamations were iſſued in one year to check this ſpirit of defection *(b)*, which was communicated even to the troops not yet embarked for the French coaſt.

THE perſevering courage and maſterly conduct of the Baſtard of Orleans con-

author) pluſieurs femmes debauchées, qui empechoient les gens d'armes de faire diligence au ſervice du roi ; quoi voyant icelle Jeanne, elle tirà ſon epée et en battît deux ou trois tant qu'elle rompît ſa dite epée : dont le roi fut bien deplaiſant, lui diſant qu'elle devoit avoir pris un *bon baton* et frapper deſſús, ſans abandonner ainſi celle epée, qui lui etoit venue devinement comme elle diſoit."

Hiſt. of Charles VII. by Jean Chatrier, p. 29 in D. Godefroy's Collection.

(b) The puniſhment inflicted on deſerters at this time was impriſonment during the king's pleaſure, with loſs of horſes and accoutrements ; but this mild penalty being found inneffectual, a law was enacted in the eighteenth of this reign, by which deſertion, after a ſoldier had once been muſtered, was made felony.—Act. Pub. and Statutes at large.

ſummated

fummated the great work which the Sect.
fortunate but fhort-lived efforts of this VII.
enterprizing heroine began. He has 1431.
been celebrated by contemporary *(c)*
writers as one of the braveft and moft
fkilful captains of his age. After having
fignalized himfelf in all the brilliant ac-
tions of this period, and wound up the
clue of his military fame by the recovery
of the whole province of Guyenne to
the French crown, he died full of years,
and to the titles of Count of Dunois and
Longue-ville added the glorious appellation of the Deliverer of his country *(d)*.

THE

(c) Chartier, De Coucy, Bouvier, and others collected and publifhed by D. Godefroy.

(d) Hall in his Chronicle, fol. 104, reports, that
this baftard was a natural fon of the duke of Orleans,
by the wife of the lord Cawny, conftable of one of the
duke's caftles on the frontier towards Artois; and that,
upon the death of his parents, the next of kin to the lord
Cawny

SECT.
VII.

1431.

THE prefence of an infant prince, to whom the inhabitants were almoft univerfally perfect ftrangers, was not likely to work any very favourable effect upon their fentiments; and Henry, after a fhort refidence in his French dominions, re-

1432.

turned, with the natural prejudice for domeftic fcenes, to his native ifland.

Cawny challenged the inheritance; that in conclufion the matter was brought before the prefidents of the parliament of Paris, and there remained in litigation till the boy was eight years of age; when, on a day appointed for a final hearing, the infant hero being afked whofe fon he was, contrary to the leffons and expectations of his mother's friends, boldly replied, " My heart giveth me and my noble courage telleth " me, that I am the fon of the noble duke of Orleans; " more glad to be his baftard with a mean living, " than the lawful fon of that cowardly cuckold " Cawny with his four thoufand crowns." A paffage which I have been induced to mention, rather from the refemblance it bears to fome circumftances in Shakefpear's interefting character of Faulconbridge, than from any conviction of its authenticity.

The

The citizens *(e)* of London teftified
their loyalty on the occafion, in a pageant
decorated with emblematical devices,
well fuited to the immature tafte and
tender age of a monarch who was then
only in his eleventh year. The archbifhop of Canterbury, at the head of his
fuffragans and the canons of St. Paul's,
received him at the door of the cathedral,
and conducted him in folemn triumph
to the great altar, where he made a devout
offering.

MARTIN, as has been obferved,
had fummoned a council to fit at Bafil,
but did not live to fee it meet. The
new pope, Eugenius the fourth, confirmed the bull granted by his predecef-
for, and the council was accordingly
convened. Its deliberations however,
the profeffed defign of which was to

(e) Fabian's Chron. p. 423 to 428.

unite

unite the Greek and Latin churches, and reform the church univerſal, did not obtain the pope's ſanction or approbation: and, after repeated differences, the fathers of the council and the Roman pontiff came to an open rupture: a mutual proſcription was the reſult. The council paſſed ſentence of depoſition againſt Eugenius, who in return declared that congregation illegal and excommunicated.

Notwithstanding theſe reciprocal diſqualifications, both parties ſtill held their ſeparate aſſemblies, and continued to aſſert their reſpective ſuperiority. It was not likely that any part of Chriſtendom ſhould remain unintereſted ſpectators of the progreſs of this controverſy: in 1431 Chichelé imparted to his ſuffragans a ſummons which he had received from the legate who preſided at Baſil, and

and recommended it to their immediate
confideration. In the next year he met his clergy in convocation at London, where, having elected fit perfons to attend the council, they affeffed the ecclefiafti-cal benefices at two pence in the pound to fupply the expences of their appoint-ment. Eugenius had by this time, from difguft at fome meafures of the council, removed it from Bafil to Bologna. Chi-chelé affembled a fynod to confult what fteps were proper to be taken at this conjuncture; when it was determined by a majority of voices to fend delegates to the pope, whom they accounted fully juftified in what he had done, as well as to the fathers at Bafil *(f)*. The depu-ties to thefe laft were directed to fupport the party which embraced the old mode

(f) Wilkins's Concil. vol. iii. p. 521, 522.

of

SECT.
VII.

1433. of voting by nations, if any thing that involved such a question should be agitated. This method would give England as great weight in the decisions of the council as any other of the four nations *(g)* singly possessed; an equality that must probably be destroyed by the superior number of agents from foreign courts, whenever the form of voting by deputies should be adopted.

THE history of some subsequent synods furnishes little matter worth remark; the clergy appear to have suffered from an unfair construction of the statute of præmunire, and to have tried the usual and ineffectual means of redress, spiritual censures. But whatever grievances the ecclesiastics might labour under, and

1434.

(g) These were Germany, France, Italy, Spain; acknowledged as such by the council of Constance.

whatever

whatever refentment they might har-
bour, their grants to the crown were
regular and competent. The inconfiderable bufinefs tranfacted in thefe provincial meetings left Chichelé more than
ordinary leifure, and this he omitted no
opportunity of improving to the advantage both of his diocefe and province. His
mind, not reftrained to the contemplation of adjacent objects, took a wider
range ; as his advanced age forbade him
to entertain a hope of continuing much
longer in the fervice of his contempora-
ries, he extended his provident care to
pofterity, and to temporary benefits added one of a more permanent duration ; in
fourteen hundred and thirty-feven he
laid the foundation of a college in Oxford : a lafting teftimony of his regard
for literature, and its beneficial influence
on fociety *(h)*.

S E C T.
VII.

1434.

1435,
1436.

1437.

(h) See next fection.

2   Eugenius

1438.

EUGENIUS having convened a fresh
council at Ferrara, Chichelé *(i)* signi-
fied to his clergy affembled in convocation this ftep, taken by the pope for the
fake, as his holinefs's letters intimated,
of facilitating the reconciliation of the
Greek and Latin Churches; in which
good work he requefted the Englifh
clergy to fecond him, by nominating
proper reprefentatives to attend the council. Thefe frequent removes of the
council which adhered to the pontiff's
intereft, and the coexiftence of another
at Bafil, whofe regulations, though condemned by the court of Rome, were too
reafonable and of too conciliating *(k)* a

(i) Wilkins's Concilia, vol. iii. p. 525.

(k) Such as the fuppreffion of the annates, one of
the moft productive branches of the papal revenues.
L'Enfant's Hift. of Council of Bafil, p. 446.

nature

nature not to find numerous advocates, augmented the charges, and divided the fentiments, of the Englifh church. It was with difficulty that a contribution was raifed adequate to the expences of the delegates chofen to this office. The fecular clergy were unalterably determin- ed againft any grant *(l)* : the monaftic orders, more devoted to the papal fee, levied the whole on their own revenues. Chichelé, whofe veneration for the head of the catholic church was ever correct- ed by a falutary regard for the conftitu- tional privileges of that part of it over which he was more immediately placed as guardian, communicated to his fuffra- gans and clergy, affembled in this fynod, an infringement of thefe privileges at- tempted by the pope in the provifion of

(l) Wilkins's Concil. vol. iii. p. 532.

a bifhop

a bishop to the vacant see of Ely : desiring their counsel and assistance in a case of so serious an importance to their community in general, and which in his own person required to be treated with a gentle yet steady and resolute hand. If a peculiarity of circumstances could have induced Chichelé to depart from the general tenour of his conduct, such an inducement was presented to him in the present instance : the inclination of his sovereign, and the distinguished merit of the candidate for this dignity, might have reconciled him to such a deviation, without fixing on him the reproach either of an unresisting ductility of temper, or of too courtly an obsequiousness of manners. The person provided by Eugenius was Lewis archbishop of Rowen, whose services *(m)* to the king in France

(*m*) Act. Pub. tom. v. pag. 53.

had

had given him a fubftantial claim to
royal favour. Powerful as this recommendation was, the irregularity of the
French prelate's appointment determined
Chichelé againft it; nor could he be prevailed upon, by any confideration, to in-
veft him with the fpiritualities of his
bifhopric *(n)*.

THE fame oppofition to papal ufur-
pations was difcovered by him in a
difpute with Kempe archbifhop of
York, who contended, that as cardinal
he ought to have precedence of him in
the houfe of peers. In the courfe of this
controverfy the pope naturally threw his
weight into the cardinal's fcale; but
Chichelé ftrenuoufly infifted, that in the.

(n) This prelate did not however remain unre-
compenfed ; the king granted him the full enjoyment
of the temporalities of the bifhopric under the title of
perpetual adminiftrator of the fee of Ely. Ibid.

K 2   character

character of cardinal, Kempe's rank and pre-eminence was derived folely from an attendance on the pontiff's perfon, and limited to the refidence of his court.

WHILE the convocation was fitting, the univerfities, which were at this pe-riod in a very reduced ftate, prefented a remonftrance, containing an ample ac-count of the grievances they laboured under, and which they attributed to the wars, want of money, and the total ne-glect of their members in the difpofal of church preferments (o). To alleviate thefe diftreffes, and remove one caufe of their complaint, Chichelé decreed, with the concurrence of the fynod, that all ecclefiaftical patrons fhould, for ten years to come, confer the benefices in their gift on members of either univerfity

(o) A. Wood. Hift. of Univ. L. i. p. 217.

exclufively;

exclufively; and that vicars general, commiffaries, and officials, fhould be chofen out of the graduates in civil and common law,

THE next convocation that Chichelé affembled he opened by an enumeration of the hardfhips the clergy fuffered, from an erroneous conftruction and undue application of the act of præmunire. After ftating the feveral abufes which had obtained under colour of enforcing this law, in terms of great energy and fenfibility, he begged the affembly to take the menacing pofture of affairs into their moft ferious confideration. The refult was a petition to the crown, that the ftatutes in queftion fhould be taken to extend only to thofe who commenced any fuits, or procured any writs or public inftruments, at Rome or elfewhere out

of

of England *(p)*, agreeable to the original purport and defign of them. Chichelé and his fuffragans prefented this
petition; and the king gracioufly anfwer-
ed, that he would have their requeft laid
before the parliament, and in the interim would give orders that no writ of
præmunire fhould be iffued till he had
in council been more fully advifed. The
augmentation of fmall vicarages was likewife fuggefted and adopted in this fynod.
The conftitution which Chichelé publifhed, for carrying fo defirable a meafure
into execution, is framed with that attention to the interefts of the inferior members of the clerical order, which befpeaks
him the common father of the whole
body. The general falary of vicars was
therein fettled by a rate proportioned

(p) Blackftone's Comment. book iv. p. 113.

both

both to the value of the rectory and the
service attending it; and no stipend less
than an annual income of twelve marks
was admitted as an adequate endowment
of a vicarage, unless the rents of the
rectory did not amount to that sum *(q)*.

THIS was the last synod Chichelé's
feeble state permitted him to attend in
person. From this time to his death he
seems, if we except the examination of
Eleanor *(r)* duchess of Glocester, to 1441.

(q) Wilkins's Conc. p. 535.

(r) The duchess of Glocester was examined before Chichelé, the cardinals Beaufort and Kempe,
and others, in St. Stephen's chapel, on a charge of
having attempted the king's life by witchcraft. The
most material circumstance relative to this affair is,
that in consequence of her condemnation a statute
passed for trying peeresses by their equals; a privilege
not extended to the wives of peers till that period.

Stowe— and Parl. History.

K 4   have

1441.

have declined all interference in public bufinefs : finking beneath the oppreffive weight of fourfcore years, and no longer equal to the fatigues which his ftation as primate impofed on him, he wifhed to refign his office into more able hands ; defirous of preparing himfelf for his approaching diffolution he languifhed for retirement. His application to Euge‑nius in fourteen hundred and forty‑two,

1442.

to obtain this indulgence, is fraught with many ftrokes of piety and goodnefs of heart. " Praife be to the living God," (fays the venerable prelate) " by whofe " bleffing I have attained to that fulnefs " of years, which has enabled me to ga‑ " ther myfelf as it were into my own bo‑ " fom, and, with a perfect indifference for " the world and its vanities, employ my " whole thoughts and care on my own " prefervation ; I am now, holy father, " heavy

" heavy laden, aged, infirm and weak
" beyond meafure; infomuch that hence-
" forth I fhall be totally unequal and
" incompetent to the charge I have
" fo long borne and ftill continue to
" bear. For the welfare, therefore, and
" fafety of that flock, which is equally
" the object of your attention as of
" mine; for my repofe and the falva-
" tion of my foul, I intreat on my
" knees, that your holinefs would re-
" leafe me from a burden I am no longer
" able to fupport either with eafe to
" myfelf or advantage to others: in
" pity then fuffer me to furrender my
" charge into your facred apoftolic
" hands; grant me a fhort refpite that
" I may bewail my infirmities; O fpare
" me a little that I may recover my
" ftrength, before I go hence and be

2 " no

" no more feen *(s)*." The archbifhop concludes this epiftle with an earneft recommendation of the bifhop of Bath for his fucceffor, whom great talents, noble birth, powerful connexions, a conciliating hofpitality, and devout zeal for the holy fee, combined to render worthy of fuch an appointment.

To Chichelé's importunities Henry condefcended to join his royal interceffion *(t)*, and particularly to urge the referve of fome fuitable provifion out of the rents of the fee of Canterbury, left that prelate might on his refignation want a fupport, which his liberal mind, ever a ftranger to the low fchemes of perfonal emolument, had, during the long

(s) See this letter in Appendix Nº I.
(t) Ibid.

enjoyment

enjoyment of that lucrative ftation, neglected to fecure. Whatever influence
thefe applications might have had on the
court of Rome, its decifions were fo
tardy that Chichelé did not live to fee
the effect of them : the month of April
1443 put a period to his life; the lefs pe-
rifhable monuments of it will be the
fubject of the next fection *(u)*.

(u) It may be proper to mention here, that in
1440 the king granted to the archbifhop and others
the alien priories to hold in fee.

Act. Pub. vol. v. p. 91.

SECTION VIII.

THE chief scenes of Chichelé's munificence were Higham-ferrers, the diocese of Canterbury, and the university of Oxford. The first of these was particularly endeared to him, as being the place of his nativity, and the residence of those who were most closely united to him by the ties of blood and affection. The second was forcibly recommended to his notice, as giving him eminence of rank and power. To the third he was indebted for the accomplishments which raised him to this rank,

and

and qualified him for the right use of this power.

In May 1422 Chichelé obtained letters patent of Henry V. to found a collegiate church at Higham-ferrers, for the maintenance of eight chaplains, four clerks, and six choristers, to pray daily for the souls of the king and queen and the archbishop, for the souls of Henry IV. and Mary his consort, for the parents of the archbishop, for his benefactors, and all faithful persons deceased. A master was to be chosen out of the chaplains to preside over the college, and two of their body, either clerks or chaplains, to teach grammar and church-music. The possessions with which Chichelé endowed this foundation were, the alien priory of Mersey in Essex, the manor of Overdene in Bedfordshire, sixty

acres

acres of woodland at Swynefhede in Hun-
tingdonfhire, the manor of Chefterton,
and Veife's manor in Bereford near New-
enham, together with thirty acres of
arable and ten of pafture land, a meffuage called *le fwan on the hope*, fixty
acres of arable and ten of meadow at
Higham-ferrers *(a)*. To thefe poffeffions Chichelé's brothers made valuable
additions; and, at the diffolution of monafteries, the clear annual income a-
mounted to one hundred and fifty-fix
pounds two fhillings and eight pence *(b)*.

This college was a quadrangular building, about fifteen yards fquare within,
having two wings projecting weftward,
and a handfome gateway on the eaft fide

(a) Monafticon Anglic. vol. iii. p. 175.
(b) Tanner's Notitia, p. 388.

with

with three niches over it *(c)*, which probably held the images of the virgin Mary, St. Thomas of Canterbury, and St. Edward the confeſſor, to whoſe patronage it was recommended *(d)*. The collegiate church is ſtill ſtanding, and ſerves for the pariſh church. Another act of Chichelé's benevolence to his native place, was the erection of an hoſpital for the poor of the town, who, beſides the broken meat they received from the college, had a daily allowance of one penny each *(e)*.

The metropolitical dioceſe is, in various parts of it, indebted to Chichelé's bounty for extenſive embelliſhments. At

(c) Anonymous authors of the Hiſtory of Northamptonſhire, vol. ii.
(d) Ibid.
(e) A. Wood. MS. Hiſt. of Univ. of Oxford.

6   Canterbury

Canterbury he expended large fums in adorning the cathedral, and in building a library which he furnifhed with a good collection of books in all kinds of learning *(f)*. At Lambeth he was a confiderable repairer and improver of the archiepifcopal palace. From the year 1424 to the year 1441, we find in his fteward's accounts mention of a variety of rooms built at his expence : but the moft important work undertaken there by this munificent prelate was the great tower, fince called the Lollard's tower. It was built in the 13th of Henry VI.

(f) Thefe benefactions were reckoned up in a public inftrument made by the prior and monks of Canterbury, and recorded among the public acts of the church, in which they promife on their part, that Chichelé's body fhould be laid in the tomb that he had caufed to be built on the north fide of the chancel, and that no one befide fhould ever be buried in that quarter.—A. Duck.

at

at the weft end of the chapel, on the fite of an old ftone edifice taken down to make room for the erection of it. All the expences of building it are particularly enumerated in the computus ballivorum, or fteward's account, of that year; whereby it appears that the total charge of the tower amounted to two hundred and feventy-eight pounds two fhillings and eleven pence *(g)*. At Croydon the parifh church was probably either erected, or received great repairs, by Chichelé's order, as the walls of the porch and fteeple bear his arms. We may here add, though it does not properly belong to the diocefe of Canter-

(g) This account of Lambeth palace is taken from a manufcript written by Dr. A. C. Ducarrel, and communicated by his permiffion.

L   bury,

bury, that he is mentioned in the lift of benefactors to Rochefter bridge *(b)*.

BUT the nobleft exertions of Chiche-lé's liberality were dedicated to the fervice of literature, and the improvement of the univerfity of Oxford; which at this time, and for fome years before, laboured under very oppreffive difcouragements. Learning was fallen into general contempt; the number of ftudents was much decreafed, and many halls totally deferted *(i)*. The ancient languages were not critically underftood; Latin, the only one of the dead tongues in common ufe, was appropriated to the unintelligible jargon of fchoolmen and meta-

(h) Stowe's Chronicle, p. 335.

(i) A. Wood. Hift. Univ. Oxon. p. 216 — he tells us that the poorer fcholars were fo deftitute, as to beg their bread from door to door.

phyficians;

phyficians; theology and philofophy
were involved in a maze of intricate and unprofitable enquiries; and even the ftudy of the civil and cánon laws, overwhelmed with endlefs commentaries, was more calculated to exercife than improve the underftanding. While genius, thus fettered by prejudice and prefcription, was idly amufed in fubtle and uninftructive refearches, the free exercife of judgment and reafon was neceffarily difcountenanced and fuppreffed. What contributed perhaps to thicken the cloud of ignorance which enveloped this period was an extreme fcarcity of books: they were purchafed at a great price, and lent with the utmoft caution and reluctance *(l)*.

L 2   T HE

(*l*) Before the invention of printing had multiplied works of literature, inftances of the jealous
spirit

SECT.
VIII.

THE manners of the ſtudents were as barbarous as their erudition. Each line, attached with bigotted partiality to their peculiar ſtudy, aſſerted its pre-eminence with intemperate zeal, and held every other branch of ſcience in ſovereign contempt. But the great factions which divided the univerſity were thoſe of the northern and ſouthern members, whoſe inveterate *(m)* prejudices and unvarying animoſity

ſpirit with which they were guarded were by no means unfrequent. In 1424 the counteſs of Weſtmoreland preſented a formal petition to the protector and council, for the reſtitution of *the Chronicles of Jeruſalem*, and *the Voyage of Godfrey of Bulloign*, which ſhe had lent to the late king. *The Works of Pope St. Gregory*, equally precious in the eſtimation of the prior of Chriſtchurch Canterbury, met, under ſimilar circumſtances, with the ſame reſpectful attention; and the council, convinced of the importance of theſe claims, gave immediate order to have them ſatisfied.
Act. Pub. tom iv. part iv. p. 105.

(m) Mr. Tyrwhit informs us, from William of Malmſbury, L. iii. Pontif. Anglic. that the language
of

animofity were difplayed on many occa-
fions in the moft violent and fanguinary
contefts *(n)*. Such was the ftate of the
univerfity, when Chichelé determined to
enlarge its eftablifhments by an addition
to the number of its colleges. He began the execution of this defign by erect-
ing a houfe for the accommodation of
the fcholars of the Ciftercian order, who
at that time had no fettled habitation in
Oxford. It was built in the north gate
ftreet, and dedicated to the Virgin Mary

of the north of England was fo harfh and unpolifhed,
as to be fcarce intelligible to a fouthern man ; " quod
" propter viciniam barbararum gentium, et propter
" remotionem regum, quondam Anglorum, modo
" Normannorum contigit, qui magis ad auftrum,
" quam ad aquilonem diverfati nofcuntur."— See
note on verfe 17354, vol. iii. Canterbury Tales.

(n) A. Wood. Hift. Univ. Oxon. lib. i. p. 194.

and

S E C T.
VIII.

and St. Bernard *(o)*. To complete the plan, which he had thus far but partially effected, the archbishop, incited to it by motives of earnest solicitude for the welfare of the church, and compassion for those who had unfortunately fallen in the French war *(p)*, erected the college of All Soulen (or All Souls) as it was commonly expressed, for the maintenance of certain persons, to pray in general for the souls of all the faithful de-

(o) This mansion, and about five acres of ground, the site and precinct of it, were granted 26th Henry VIII. to the dean and chapter of Christchurch, who alienated them in the reign of Philip and Mary to Sir Thomas White; and by him they were made a part of the college which he erected, and dedicated to St. John the Baptist. —

Stevens's Monasticon, vol. ii. p. 52.

(p) MS. Statutes in Archives of A. S. Coll.

ceased

ceafed *(q)*, and who might increafe the number of the minifters of religion, and promote by their ftudies the knowledge of theology and of the civil and canon law.

THE firft purchafe *(r)* for the fite of this college was made on the 14th of

(q) They were more efpecially to pray for the good eftate of Henry VI. and the archbifhop during their lives, and for their fouls after their deceafe; alfo for the fouls of Henry V. and the duke of Clarence, together with thofe of all the dukes, earls, barons, knights, efquires, and other fubjects of the crown of England who had fallen in the war with France.—See Chart of Incorp. Appendix Nº IV.

(r) The piece of ground conveyed to the college by this purchafe was one hundred and feventy-two feet in length, and one hundred and fixty-two in breadth, meafured from the corner neareft to the eaft end of St. Mary's church, and contained a meffuage called Bereford Hall, and fix fhops—Ibid.

The fite was enlarged by the purchafe of fome additional tenements and ground adjoining, during the progrefs of the building, which are particularly fpecified in the Appendix N• IV.

L 4

December

December 1437, by Thomas Chichelé
archdeacon of Canterbury, Henry Penwortham, clerk, and Robert Danvers,
feoffees to the ufe of the archbifhop.
The building was begun under the in-
fpection of John Druell, clerk, on the
10th of February in the fame year *(s)*.
In the May following the charter of
foundation was publifhed by letters patent, in which the king, at the folicitation *(t)* of the archbifhop, takes upon
himfelf the title of founder: the full
exercife of legiflative authority, and every

(s) Original deeds in Archiv. of A. S. C.

(t) Chichelé has given his reafon for foliciting
the king's patronage as founder in the following
words; " Sic enim fperavimus quod eo felicius pium
" hoc noftræ intentionis propofitum ad optatum per-
" veniret effectum, fecuriufque ac quietius in perpe-
" tuum confifteret, quo ipfum tantæ majeftatis regiæ
" fpeciale patrocinium muniret."
Preface to Statutes in Archiv. of A. S. C.

other

other eſſential right belonging to that character, being ſtill reſerved to the archbiſhop, under the deſcription of co-founder.
By this charter a warden and twenty fellows, of Chichele's election, are firſt appointed, and a power lodged in the
warden *(u)* of augmenting the ſociety
to the number of forty. The charter
then grants them, by the name of *The
Warden and College of the Souls of all the
Faithful deceaſed,* a common ſeal, and the
other uſual privileges of corporate bodies. Of the whole ſociety thus conſti-

(u) By the ſtatutes Chichelé transfers this power
from the warden to the fellows of the college; a cir-
cumſtance that gave riſe to a diſpute in the ſociety
ſoon after his death, ſome of the original members
urging that the warden's appointment was contrary
to the ſtatutes: upon an appeal to archbiſhop Staf-
ford the viſitor, he confirmed the warden's nomination, as authorized by the charter of foundation before any ſtatutes were made.—See chart. in Appendix; and Regiſt. 1ſt, fol. 103, in Archiv. of A. S. C.

tuted,

tuted, fixteen were to ftudy the civil and canon laws, and the reft were to apply themfelves to philofophy (or the arts) and theology. The names of the firft twenty fellows are given in the note below *(w)*. The perfon to whom he committed the government of his new foundation is, from that confideration, intitled to more particular mention.

(w)	
Tho' Lavenham,	Rob' Karewe,
Tho' Vauge,	Simon Hoore,
Tho' Winterbourne,	John Julyan,
Rob' Hoo,	Walter Hopton,
James Laye,	Rob' Stephens,
Rich. Le Toft,	Rob' Seburgh,
Wm Horneden,	Wm Overton,
John Gygour,	Tho' Efton,
John Porter,	Rich. Warde,
Walter Hart,	Rich. Penwortham.

The chaplains, though not mentioned in the charter, appear by the ftatutes to have been a part of the original foundation.—See Statutes in A. S. C. library.

RICHARD

RICHARD ANDREWS had been some years fellow of New College, where he had studied the civil and canon law with the success due to good natural abilities and diligent application, when archbishop Chichelé removed him to the wardenship of his college of All Souls *(x)*. This trust he discharged for the space of four years, with a zeal and fidelity in the highest degree satisfactory to his patron,

---

(x) If gratitude to a society of which he had formerly been a member may not be thought a sufficient motive to have directed Chichelé to this choice, the following note from the Stemmata Chicheleana suggests one by no means improbable; " In the year 1558 a person of the name and family of Andrews " (John Andrews) was elected fellow as kinsman of " the founder ; and from this circumstance perhaps " we may be allowed to suppose that Richard Andrews, " whom the archbishop appointed the first warden " of his new foundation, and who was his great favourite, might be of the same family and his near " relation."—See Stemmat. Chichelean. p. 155.

who

who, as a further mark of the confidence he repofed in him, appointed him one of his executors *(y)*. In 1442 he refigned the wardenfhip, and was from that time employed in a more confpicuous ftation. Befides ecclefiaftical preferments of confiderable value, he enjoyed the honourable poft of fecretary to the king, in which capacity he bore a great part in moft of the treaties of this reign, and was particularly diftinguifhed by the charge of attending Margaret of Anjou in France, and when fhe came to fhare the Englifh throne. Towards the clofe of his life he renewed his connection with the college, the members of which, in confideration of various gifts of copes,

---

(y) He appears to have been auditor to the archbifhop in 1437, but whether prior to his being warden I am not able to afcertain.

Tanner's Biblioth. article Chichelé.

chalices,

chalices, and books, as well as money S ᴇ ᴄ ᴛ.
expended in their buildings, admitted .VIII.
him a brother of their fociety, engaged
to celebrate his obit annually, and to give
on the day preceding four pence to the
bellman of the city, to invite by proclamation all good chriftians to offer up a
prayer for his foul.

Tʜᴇ king's authority was certainly
fufficient in point of law to create a cor-
poration; but Chichelé, to render the
eftablifhment unexceptionable, thought
it neceffary, according to the fuperftition
of the age, to obtain the pope's confirmation. With this view he fent Richard
Andrews to Eugenius IV. then at Flo-
rence, with a tranfcript of the charter of
foundation duly attefted under the feal
of the court of arches; and that pon-

tiff

tiff readily granted a bull to confirm it *(z)*.

THE buildings of the college were in the mean time carried on without interruption : the archbiſhop had frequent interviews with the ſurveyor, and, though now very old and infirm, came ſeveral times to Oxford to inſpect in perſon the progreſs of his foundation *(a)*. In 1442 the building was ſufficiently advanced for the reception of the warden and fellows, who ſince their incorporation had been maintained and

(z) The tranſcript bears date July 1430, the bull of confirmation July 1439.—In Archiv. of A. S. C.

(a) It appears from the following entry in the *rationarium fundationis* that the archbiſhop reſided, during theſe viſits, at the monaſtery of South Oſney ; " Idem reſpondet de 12ᵃ. receptis de ſeneſchallo domini Cantuarenſis pro quatuor carectis fœni ſibi " venditis ad uſum domini Cantuar. apud Oſeney.

6   lodged,

lodged, at the archbifhop's expence, in a hall and divers chambers hired for that purpofe *(b)*. The exact time when they made their entrance is no where fpecified; but it was probably in the fpring, for the chapel was confecrated early in the year. The archbifhop himfelf performed this folemn ceremony, affifted by the bifhops of Lincoln, Worcefter, Norwich, and other fuffragans *(c)*. By the bull of pope Eugenius, in confirmation of the king's charter, authority had been given to the college to erect a chapel and place of burial within their own precincts. By virtue of the fame autho-

---

(b) Pro locatu unius aulæ et diverfarum camerarum cum coquinâ et ftabulis, 15°.—Ibid

(c) Hoc anno (1442) vifitationi ecclefiæ omnium animarum collegii interfuerunt Henricus Cantuar. fundator, Wilhelm. Lincoln, T. S. Wigorne, T. Norwicen. et alii fuffraganei.— Senior proctor's book.

rity

rity the fellows were exempted from the
obligation of attending divine fervice at
the parochial church of St. Mary, and
from the payment of all contributions
to it *(d)*. This exemption Chichelé
ratified by a compromife with Oriel
college *(e)* as proprietaries of the faid
church.

The chapel was dedicated to the four
fathers, Jerom, Ambrofe, Auftin, and
Gregory ; and the firft mafs was celebrated with the ufual folemnities in May,
four years after the incorporation of the

(*d*) See bull of pope Eugenius, Appendix, Nº V.

(*e*) This compromife, by which Oriel college was
to receive 200 marks in the place of all ecclefiaftical
dues whatever, was afterwards executed by indenture
between Walter Lyhert provoft and the fellows of
Oriel on one part, and Roger Keys warden and the
fellows of A. S. C. on the other, dated November
1443.—In Archiv. of A. S. C.

fociety.

society. The whole of the building was not finished before the latter end of 1444. The expences of it, as accurately stated by John Druell *(f)*, and Roger Keys his succeffor in the office of furveyor, amounted to £. 4,156. 5s. 3¼d. If to this fum we add the amount of the purchafes made by the feoffees to the archbifhop's ufe within the fame period, which, including books and other neceffary articles for the fervice of the college, is ftated at £. 4,302. 3s. 8d. we fhall

---

(f) John Druell was elected fellow of the college 1440, was collated to the archdeaconry of Exeter 1443, and prefented by the college to the living of Harrietfham a fhort time after.—See 1ft Regift. in Archiv. of the Coll. and Le Neve's Fafti, p. 93.

Roger Keys had the fupervifion of the building in the fifth and fubfequent year : he was made fellow 1438, and fucceeded R. Andrews as warden 1442. Under the immediate direction of thefe two perfons the edifice of the college was erected.

M   obtain

Sᴇᴄᴛ.
VIII.

obtain a competent notion of the liberal
fpirit with which the archbifhop provided for his new foundation *(g)*.

Tнᴇ valuable, though comparatively
fmall, donations of £. 123. 6s. 8d. *(h)*
to New College, and of an equal fum to
the univerfity cheft, as a fund for fmall
loans to the members, are teftimonies of
his condefcending attention to the ac-
commodations of a ftudious life, in the
moft minute inftances. To the public
library, then juft founded by the duke of
Glocefter, he not only contributed largely

(g) Rationarium fundationis in Archives of
A. S. C. which contains a very full and accurate
account of all the fums of money expended on the
buildings of the college, as delivered in annually by
the furveyors.

(h) A. Wood. Hift. Univ. Oxon. vol. ii.

himfelf,

himſelf, but ſolicited a ſubſcription towards it from all the biſhops and peers
who came to the parliament at Weſtminſter *(i)*.

HAVING built his college and endowed it with adequate revenues *(i)*, his
laſt care was to furniſh the ſociety with
a code of ſtatutes, which he did not
tranſmit to them till within a few days
of his death; having determined that it
ſhould be as perfect as deliberate conſi-
deration and frequent reviſion could render it. This code is evidently modelled
after the ſtatutes of New College, and is
ſuppoſed to have been the compoſition
of the famous civilian Lyndewode *(k)*,
under the archbiſhop's inſpection. The

(*i*) A. Wood. Hiſt. Univ. Oxon. vol. ii.
(*k*) The ſame who has been mentioned as prolo-
cutor of the lower houſe of convocation.

M 2   founder

founder fet his feal to it on the 2d of April 1443; on the 12th he died, in the thirtieth year of his adminiftration of the metropolitan fee, and about the eighty-firft of his life.

HIS remains were depofited on the north fide of the choir of the cathedral of Canterbury; where, upon a monument erected in his life, lies his effigy robed in the pontifical veftments, and beneath it a fkeleton in a fhrowd *(l)*. By his laft will he bequeathed to the college £. 133. 6*s.* 8*d.* and 1000 marks. Thefe legacies were duly paid *(m)* by his executors, Thomas Chichelé *(n)*, archdeacon of Canterbury, Richard Andrews, William Byconyll, John Birkhede, Robert

(l) See Dart's Antiquities of Canterbury.
(m) See Charters in Archives of the College.
(n) Thomas Chichelé was grandfon of William the

Robert Danvers, and John Wraby. He
left likewife an annuity of feven pounds
to be paid by the college to the prior
and convent of Canterbury; who in return bind themfelves to perform maffes
for his foul, and to light up wax candles
before his fepulchre *(o)*.

the archbifhop's brother, and was collated to the archdeaconry 14th of December 1433.

Stemmat Chichel. pref.
Richard Andrews has been already mentioned.

John Birkhede appears to have been fteward to the
archbifhop. He was admitted a brother of the college in 1465, and as fuch became intitled to the be-
nefit of their prayers and other fpiritual exercifes.

1ft Regifter, fol. 11 and 19.
John Wraby was entrufted with feveral fums for
the payment of the workmen during the building of
the college, and is mentioned in the lift of its benefactors.—

Rationarium Fund. and Deeds in the Archives.
Robert Danvers was a feoffee to the archbifhop.
Of Wm Byconyll no mention is made but as executor.

(o) From Charters in the Archives.

WE

WE have now feen Chichelé in the feveral fituations in which a long and active life placed him. It is from his conduct in thefe that we are to collect his character. Of the early part of his life we know little more, than that his acquirements in it are indifputable proofs of his not having paffed it unpro-fitably.

As he grew into public notice by flow and gradual advances, his talents had time to acquire their full ftrength and maturity before they were brought into ufe: and it is to this circumftance probably that he owes the uninterrupted courfe of his fuccefs in the management

of

of repeated negotiations. As he was able to acquit himself in these important commissions with the favour of his sovereign, and the approbation of his country, we may infer, that he possessed, besides extensive erudition, clear discernment, fertility of resources, solid judgment, and cool perseverance, recommended by general urbanity and politeness of manners. If we view him in the discharge of his ecclesiastical office, we shall find him to have been a man of undissembled piety, and who bore a sincere affection to the church. If his religion was tinctured with the superstition of the times in which he lived, we should recollect, that in passing judgment on the characters of men, we ought to try them by the maxims and principles of their own age.

FULLY

Fᴜʟʟʏ perſuaded of the truth of thoſe doctrines which the catholic church profeſſed, he maintained them with conſcientious zeal. He knew the danger of innovation, and was vigilant to repreſs it; but he does not at any time appear to have been actuated by the ſpirit of perſecution *.

Tʜᴏᴜɢʜ warmly attached to the authority of the ſee of Rome in ſpiritual matters, and even to its exerciſe of civil rights founded on ancient uſage, he ſtill ſtrenuouſly ſupported the liberties of the Engliſh church, and never forgot the

* It ſhould be remembered, that when in his provincial ſynods he condemned ſeveral perſons for holding heretical tenets, he did it in his judicial capacity, not as an act of his own; the law of the realm had fixed the puniſhment, he only pronounced the ſentence of that law.

reſpect

refpect due to the laws and conftitution S E C T. VIII. of his country. Thus the doctrines and the privileges of the church were guarded by him with fcrupulous fidelity; and, in whatever light we fee his religion, there will fcarcely be two opinions concerning his integrity.

Of his benefactions a particular account has already been given; and if in fumming up his character, to excellent natural abilities, liberal accomplifhments, and ftrict piety and integrity, we add a charitable and benevolent heart, we fhall not be guilty of exceffive or blind partiality to his memory.

APPENDIX,

APPENDIX,

APPENDIX, N° I,

MS. Lamb. N° 211.
Ex epiſtolarum Thomæ Beckington,
Libro   fol. 53.

Epiſtola HENRICI CHICHLEY, *Cant. Ar-
chiepiſcopi, ad Papam.*

POST humiliores quas ulla creatu-
rarum Domino ſuo præſtare poterit
obedientias, ac terræ oſcula ante pedes,
dimittite me, beatiſſime pater, ut plangam paululum dolorem meum antequam
vadam, ut recogitem annos meos in ama-
ritudine animæ meæ. Non iraſcatur
quæſo ſanctitas veſtra, ſi, cùm pulvis et

cinis

cinis fim, domino meo loquar. Loquar quidem, quoniam ipfa fides, quam femper in dulciffimâ benignitate veftrâ repofui, nequaquam finit, ut quæ corde gero à facie patris abfcondam. Pater benigniffime, pofteaquam plufculum quam fex annos in adminiftratione Menevenfis ecclefiæ confummavi, viginti jam et octo funt anni, quod fanctam fedem Cantuarienfis ecclefiæ, licet minifter indignus, prout ex alto mihi datum eft, vexi; et nunc octogenarius aut circiter vigeffimum nonum minifterii dictæ metropoliticæ fedis annum ingredior, multis quidem oneribus et curis, quæ fæculo meo humeris meis portavi, fractus atque fatigatus. Laus Deo viventi, qui in hanc ufque annofam ætatem vivere mihi dederit, in quâ me poffum in finum meum colligere, in quâ, fpretis omnibus mundi curis, meipfum intueri curareque poffim.

Imperfectum

Imperfe&um meum fatis jam vident oculi mei. Onuftus quidem, grandævus, infirmus atque fupra modum debilis, ego nunc fum, pater beatiffime, ita ut, ex nunc maximè atque confertiffimè quam geffi et gero curæ, impar omnino et impos atque ineptus officiar. Pro falute igitur et falvâ deinceps cuftodiâ ovilis mei immo veftri, pro falute meâ et quiete animæ deinceps meæ, hanc mihi gratiam ex benignitate veftrâ provolutis genibus pofco, hanc humillime deprecor et votis omnibus concupifco, ut beatitudo veftra fenii quo premor, impotentiæque ac invalitudinis meæ, miferta, non amplius ad id quod utilitèr quod commodè fubire nequeo onus alligatum me teneat. Det ipfa mihi miferatio veftra in facras manus apoftolicas liberam cedendi licentiam, det fpatium refpirandi, det tempus (ut primò exorfus fum) ut plangam pau-

lulum

Iulum dolorem meum, antequam vadam,
et recogitem annos meos. Revolvam
numerum dierum meorum, ut fciam quod
defit mihi. Paucitas quidem dierum
meorum finitur brevi. Remitte mihi
igitur, pater fanctiffime, ut refrigerer
priufquam abeam et amplius non ero.
Hæc cogor in confcientiâ, fanctiffime
pater, idcirco petere, idcirco defiderare,
ne, ultimis diebus his meis, et in hoc
ævo imbecillitatis atque extremæ debili-
tatis meæ, pro defectu paftoris idonei,
qui valeat et velit invigilare fuper gre-
gem fuum, ampla nimis provincia Cantuarienfis luporum, quod abfit, exponatur
moribus; neve fancta fedes illa, quæ fedes fanctorum effe confueverat, injuriam
aliquam periculumve aut grave aliquod
difpendium per incuriam patiatur. Pof-
tremone videam oculis aliquando meis
ingratâ quâvis oblivione, incuriâ feu ne-
glectu

glectu fponfam hanc fanctam, quam tanto tempore fub gratiâ fedis apoftolicæ
gubernavi, jam viduam diu aut defertam
relinqui; en facio quod eft meum, et
fidenter ac fecure in teftimonio confcien-
tiæ meæ cariffimum fratrem meum Johannem Bathon. epifcopum, regni Angliæ cancellarium, ut patrem maximè me-
ritum, et pro utilitatibus dictæ fanctæ
fedis, fi univerfa virtutum dona, quæ in
eo concurrunt, quæque non dubito fanctitati veftræ nota effe debent, penfentur,
fummè neceffarium, ad præfidentiam
ejufdem fanctæ fedis beatitudini veftræ
humiliter recommendo. Profecto fi, præter eminentem fcientiam fuam et cæteras
virtutum dotes, quibus faciliter reliquos
fuperat, nobilitatem fanguinis, potentiam
amicorum neceffariorumque fuorum, ac
hofpitalitatis gratiam, in dicto patre
probè attendimus; fi devotionem, fidem,

2   obedientiam,

obedientiam, zelum, et follicita quæ fanctæ fedi Romanæ atque almæ perfonæ fanctitatis veftræ femper devotè ante hæc fecit et jugiter facit obfequia, pro confervatione honoris dignitatifque veftræ ac jurium et libertatum prædictæ fedis, bene confideramus ; non puto facile inveniri poffe, qui ufquequaque in aptitudine, habilitate et merito, ad tantum regimen commodè fubeundum meritis fibi poffit æquari. Commifi demum, benigniffimè pater, fecreta quædam induftriæ atque fidei dilecti mihi in Chrifto magiftri Thomæ Chapman veftræ beatitudinis

referenda. Et quæfo eadem beatitudo audientiam donare et fidem. Oro quoque, et inceffanter orabo dum vivam, ipfam beatitudinem veftram incolumem et falvam in multa confervet fecula, qui omnem dat falutem et falvat fperantes in fe. Script. fub annulo

S. Thomæ

3. Thomæ martyris in manerio meo de Lambeth menfis Aprilis die decima anno Dom. M CCCC XLII.

Preces Regiæ Domino Papæ tranfmiffæ pro eâdem admittendâ refignatione, et commendatio magna ipfius patris et fui regiminis pro tempore fuæ incumbentiæ.

f. 54.

CUM omni devotione filiali humil-limâ recommendatione præmiffâ, fanctiffime pater, ipfum quod agreffuri jam fumus negotium magnum certè at-que mirabilem intra nos conflictum parit. Adeò ut, propter pugnantes in mente caufas, idipfum quod devotè petituri fu-mus velle et non velle videri poffumus. Neque mirum: dum enim ad varias con-

N fiderationes

fiderationes animum flectimus, in contra-
rias pene trahimur voluntates. Ecce
enim affiduè et inceffanter nos rogat, et
maximis precum inftanter defatigat, antif-
tes et Deo et nobis cariffimus, devotif-
fimus filius vefter, Henricus Cant. Archiepifcopus, ut pro impetranda apud
fanctitatem veftram fuæ dignitati curæ
Archipontificali in facras manus veftras
cedendi licentiâ, precibus fuis addamus
et noftras. In iftam facile fententiam
pietas et compaffio grandævitatis debili-
tatifque fuæ nos trahunt. In adverfum
verò utile ac fummè laudabile et pacifi-
cum femper regimen, quo à primo limine
ingreffûs fui, jam viginti et octo funt anni, provinciam fuam rexit, nos movet.
Profectò nullis unquam temporibus fedem Cant. ecclefiæ occupare vifus eft,
qui facro-fanctæ Romanæ ecclefiæ et
præfidentibus in ea, atque fanctiffimæ
perfonæ

perfonæ veftræ, dignitatique et honori
ejufdem, fidelior aut devótior extiterit;
neque quifquam qui benignior pater
fuerit, aut benignius, fuavius, dulcius,
tranquillius, provinciam illam modera-
verit. Sed vincit nos pietas. Dum enim
-maximam fenectutem, et, quæ femper fe-
nio cognata eft, debilitatem hujus carif-
fimi patris contemplamur ad oculum,
miferatione quâdam interiora noftra li-
quefcunt; et cum jam onus tantæ curæ
per tot annorum curricula, ita ut jam vi-
geffimus nonus annus tranflationis fuæ ad
fedem præfatam in foribus aftet, probif-
fimè gefferit; neque alium quempiam
pene meminerimus qui fedem S. Thomæ
tot rexerit annis; juftum plane et bene
congruum atque Deo placabile judica-
mus, quòd jam parcatis ætati, ut vel
aptum aliquod fpatium refpirandi, et
fancto fe otio conferendi, aliquando ha-

beat,

beat, qui in laboribus, in vigīliis, in ærumnis, tantæ curæ, tanti oneris, tot fæcula trivit. Propterea, benigniſſime atque clementiſſime pater, rem hanc quam poſtulat exaudire dignemini, ut vel in feneƈute bonâ ex nunc pace fruatur, qui omni fæculo fuo omnibus pacem dedit. Precamur demum, quatenus, conceſſâ hujufmodi cedendi licentiâ, quamprimum ceſſio ipfa fuerit per fanƈitatem veſtram admiſſa, de portione congruâ ex præfatâ Cant. ecclefiâ diƈto reverendiſſimo patri annuatim quoad vixerit reddenda, de quâ ſtatum fuum honorificè fuſtentare queat, cum nullum aliunde patrimonium nofcatur habere, eadem fanƈitas veſtra providere velit : quodque de memorata Cantuarienfi, necnon Bathon et Sarum ecclefiâ, juxta deliberationem mentis noſtræ in certis aliis noſtris defuper confcriptis literis, et fecreto noſtro

aquilæ

aquilæ figneto fignatis apertis declara-
tam, quas dilectus et fidelis procurator
noſter, M. Andreas Hole, eidem fanctitati
veſtræ præſentaturus eſt, et nullo aliter
modo, ipſa beatitudo veſtra, ad benignos
et præcordiales rogatus hos noſtros, or-
dinet atque diſponat. Et almam perſo-
nam ejuſdem fanctitatis veſtræ, omnipo-
tens Pater, in multa oramus fæcula ſalvam
et incolumem eccleſiæ ſuæ conſervare
dignetur. Scriptum apud caſtrum noſtrum de Wyndeſorâ, ſub figneto noſtro
viceſimâ quartâ die Aprilis anno Domini M CCCC XLII.

APPEN-

APPENDIX, N° II.

Excusatio Cantuariensis Archiepiscopi su-
per Dilatione et Criminatione ejusdem
per Æmulos suos Papæ factis.

A p p.
II.

BEATISSIME pater, &c. misera-
bilis mundi in maligno positi in-
fælix ista conditio ubique pene inolita
est, ut obtrectatorum malitia venenosos
invidiæ suæ stimulos superbâ quadam
præsumptione exerceat in majores; et
quanto innocentioris sunt vitæ, potioris-
que authoritatis et fidei resplendeant dig-
nitate, tanto crudeliùs celebrem eorum
opinionem serpentinis a tergo quærunt
et satagunt morsibus lacerare. Quocunque me verto, quantumlibet bene gesta

componam,

componam, mordaces canum hujufmodi
dentes excipio; et, quod durum eft,
quicquid ftudiofè et curâ pervigili conor
in bonum id totum perverfâ interpreta-
tione in contrarium tranfponunt, qui
fupra dorfum meum fabricant affidue
pifcatores. Nuper fiquidem, benigniffime pater, non abfque cordîs amaritudi-
ne pro maximâ, audivi et didici, quod
quidem Jacobus, dudum cum litteris
fanctitatis veftræ ad dominum noftrum
regem et reverendiffimum in Chrifto patrem et dominum D. Cardinalem Angliæ
ab eâdem fanctitate tranfmiffus, ea quæ
ego et cæteri quidem in regno cum omni
maturitate et circumfpectione optimo
more noftro agere nifi fumus, prave
interpretans, et valde male reportans,
non erubuit etiam in facrâ beatitudinis
veftræ audientiâ fuggerendo pervertere et
pervertendo fuggerere, licet falfò, quod ubi.

N 4 clerus

clerus Angliæ in extirpatione hæretico-
rum Bohemiæ quoddam notabile fubfi-
dium concuffiffet, confrater meus Ebo-
racenfis et ego cæterique epifcopi de regis concilio exiftentes, votum ipforum
in hac parte confpiravimus et procuravi-
mus impedire ; tam fanctam et toti
Chriftianitati profuturam fidei expeditio-
nem quantum in nobis extitit irrumpen-
do ; quodque idem confrater meus et
ego, cum certis prælatis ad regis confi-
lium affumptis, cæteros de concilio do-
minos temporales conducimus prout li-
bet ; et breviter, quod nemo crederet nifi
infaniret, quod nos totum regnum Angliæ, ut volumus, gubernamus. Appo-
fuit peccare adhuc ille arrofor meus, et,
quod nefandum eft impudentèr afferere,
quod fæpe dictus confrater meus et ego in
Angliâ libertatum ecclefiæ præmaximi
oppreffores. Benigniffime pater, non-
nunquàm

nunquàm, cùm tot tantifque æmulorum A P P. II. latratibus infeſtor, et oblocutionibus in- volvor, longe amplius mente conſterna- rer ; niſi Deus et conſcientia, immo et ipſe mundus, aſſiſterent innocentiæ meæ teſtes ; niſi inſuper ſatis adverterem, quod nil præter ſolam miſeriam ſit invi- dia cariturum. Nuper detraxere mihi majores. Nunc autem per inferiores de- trahor et diſtrahor in immenſum ; et ta- men in his omnibus non peccavi, ſed conſtanter in cunctis quæ mendaces viri conati ſunt mihi impingere, meam au- deo innocentiam jactitare, et eandem tàm regis quam omnium fide dignòrum regni teſtimonio edocere. Immo et ipſæ rei geſtæ veritas ſe loquitur, ſe oſtendit. Nihil equidem in negotio præfati ſubſi- dii factum eſt omnino abſque conſcientia reverendiſſimi patris cardinalis prædicti, cujus conſilio et aſſenſu dirigebantur omnia

omnia quæ fiebant. Cum etenim, colla-
tis in unum arduis, primo fidei, deinde
et regni negotiis, devotus clerus hinc
vestris contra perfidos Bohemos, hinc
regiis contra insurgentes et malignantes
in injuriam coronæ suæ urgeretur præ-
ceptis ; responsumque fuisset per consi-
lium domini nostri regis, quod in tantâ
regni necessitate idem dominus cardinalis
vel gentibus de Angliâ vel solis pecuniis
eligeret contentari ; cum deliberatione
dixit se magis hac vice gentibus indi-
gere, et de his velle sanctitati vestræ amplius complaceri : et idcirco ne desideria
sanctitatis vestræ effectu frustrarentur ac-
commodo, de advisamento dicti domini
cardinalis convocationem in eo quo tunc
statu erat continuavi usque in et ad cras-
tinum S. Lucæ proximè secuturum : ut
interim præfato domino cardinali de gentibus expedito, posset tunc liberius de

subsidio

subfidio abfque dictæ expeditionis impe-
dimento concludi, et veftræ fanctitatis
bene placitis inferviri. Hæc, pater beatiffime, dilationis caufa extiterat; de qua
idem dominus cardinalis toti tunc clero
promiferat, fe velle per fcripta fua beatitudinem veftram fideliter informare.

A P P E N-

A P P E N D I X, N° III.

Letter of Archbishop Chichelé to King Henry.

From A. Duck's Life.

SOVEREYN Lord, as your humble Preſt and devout Bedeman, I recommand me to your Hygneſſe, deſyreing evermore to heare and knowe of your gracious ſpeed, hele of body and of foule, alſo my Lordys your brethren and all your royal hoſte. And as hertly as I can, or may thanke Almightie God and Lord of all ſtrengths and hoſtes that ſo gracioufly hath continued his mygty hond upon you ſythen the time of your beginning hedirtoward into your moſt worſhip,

worſhip, your Leige menys moſt hertly

gladneſſe, and abating of the hy pride of
your enemies. And beſech God both
day and night with all your ſubgetts
both ſpirituel and temporel ſo continue
his hy Grace upon you and yowre that
the mow come to the effect of your hy
labor, pees of both your regmes after
your hertly deſires. Gracious Lord like
it to remember you that be your moſt
worthie letters written at your towne of
Caen xxv. day of September you charged
me, that be the avys of my Lord your
brother of Bedford, and of your Chaunceler ſholde be ordeygned that all maner
of men of your ſubgets wat aſtaat or
condicion that thei were ſhould abſtyne
letter of wrytes or purſuit making to
the Pope after his election, till the time
that he have written to you, and ye againe

to

to him, as it hath be acuſtumed of ho-
neſte of your lond. for the which cauſe
neither I, nor non odir man as ferforth
as it may be knowe, hath yit written
nor ſent, ne no leve hath of paſſage to
the Cowrte, wow it ſo be that many
lych at London to purſue to my Lord
your brother, your Chaunceler, and your
Counſeil for to have leve and letters of
paſſage. Werfore Soverain Lord my
Lord your brother charged me write
to you, and in as miche aſ your letter
forſeid was direct to me, to wite, in
wat wife we ſhol governe us hereafter,
for if ye have reſteyned our holy faders
letters, or written to him it is unknowen
to us unto this time. Like it therefore,
gracious Lord, to write to my Lord
your brother in wat maner wife this matier ſchal be governed hereafter.

Forthermore

Forthermore gracious Lord, of trowth that I am bound to you be my ligeaunſe, and alſo to quite me to God, the chirch of your lond, of the wich God and, ye gracious Lord, have maked me governor, howeth to open to you this matier that ſuyeth, of the wich I have herd privily, but now it is more opend, and in ſuch wiſe that credence ſhold bee yive to by reſon; that is to ſeyne, that my brother of Wincheſter ſhold be maked a Cardinal, if ye wold give your aſent thereto, and that he ſhold have his Biſhoprich in comende for terme of his life, and therto have a ſtat, and ſent to your rengme of Yngland as a legat a latere, to the wich manier of legacie non hath be acuſtumed to be named but Cardinals, and that legacie alſo to ocupie thorgh all your obeyſaunce, and all the time of his life. Sovereyn Lord and moſt Chriſtien Prince,

what

what inftanfe fchall be maad to your Higneffe for this matier, I wot not, but bleffyd be Almightie God undir your worthie protection, your Chirche of Yngland is at this day, I dare boldly fay, the mooft Honorable Chirche Chriftien as weel as devin fervife, as honeft living thereof, governed after ftreit lawes, and holy conftitutions, that be maad of hem withowten any gret exorbitaunfes, or any thing that migt torne to hy fklaundre of your forfeid Chirch, or of your lond, and if any trefpafes of mannys frelte falleth we may be corectid and punifhed by the Ordinaries there as the caas falleth. But wat that this offis of legacie to be ocupied in the forme aforfeid, and fuich comendis of Bifhopriches not ufed in your holy Aunfetres time here afore, wold extend to, or gendre ageines the good governanfe of your fubgets, in your

hy

hy wisdom I trist to God ye will consi-
der. And forafmich as ye fchal be en-
formid what the office of fuych manier
of legacie extendith to; and appyly your
Clerkys have not in minde, for it hath
fhelde be feyn, and have not alle here
bookys with hem pleynly to enforme
you in this time of your grete labor, I
fend you a fcrowe writen with inne this
letter conteyning that is expreffed in the
Popis lawe, and fully concludyd be Doctors. And over that what he may have
in fpecial of the Popis grace no man
wot, for it ftond in his wille to difpofe
as hym good liketh. And be infpec-
tion of lawes and cronicles was there
never no Legat a latere fent in to no lond,
and fpecially into your rengme of Yngland withowte grete and notable caufe.
And thei whan thei came after thei had

O   done

done her legacie abiden but lytul wyle, not over a yer, and fumme a quarter, or two monethes, as the nedes requeryd: And yit over that he was tretyd with, or he cam into the lond whon he fchold have exercife of his power, and how myche fchold be put in execucion. An aventure after he had be refeyved he whold have ufed it to largely to greet oppreffion of your peple. Wherefore mooft Criftien Prince and Sovereyn Lord, as your trewe Preeft, whom it hath lyked you to fette in fo hy aftaat, the wych with owte your gracious Lordfhip, and fupportation I know my felf infuf-ficient to ocupie. befeche you in the mooft humble wyfe that I can devife or thenke that ye wile this matier take ten-dirly at herte, and fee the ftaat of the Chirche be meyntenid and fufteynid, fo that

that everich of the Minifters theroffe
hold hem content with her owne part:
for trewly he that hath leeft hath inow
to rekene fore: And that your poore
pepul be not pyled, nor oppreffyd with
diverfe exactions and unacuftumed, thorgh
wych thei fchold be the more feble to
refrefche you owre liege Lord in time of
nede and when it lyketh you to clepe up
on hem, and alle plees and fklaundre cefe
in your Chirche.

Towchinge oure holy fadir the Popis
Ambaffiat that late cam in to your lond,
I wot wel my Lord your brother wryt-
eth to you pleynly, and alfo of odir gq-
vernance of your lond, the wych bleffed
be God ftond in good quiet pees and
refte withowte any grete ryotis or de-
batys and al your trewe peple have her
herys opyn to here good tydinges of you

O 2 and

A P P.
III.

and continuely pray for your profperite and al yowrys, the wych Almighty God graunte for his mercy Amen. wryten at Lambyth vi day of March.

Your Preft. H. C.

Indorfed, *Au Roy noftre Souverein, S.*

APPENDIX,

APPENDIX, N° IV.

1. *Charta Fundationis.*

HENRICUS Dei gratiâ rex Angliæ et Franciæ et dominus Hi-
berniæ omnibus ad quos præfentes literæ
pervenerint falutem. Supplicavit. nobis
venerabilis pater Henricus Chichele Cantuariæ archiepifcopus, totius Angliæ pri-
mas et compater nofter, per cujus manus
facri baptifmatis lavacrum fufcepimus,
incrementum cleri regni noftri Angliæ
defiderans, qui in præfentiarum nofcitur
plurimum defeciffe; ut nos cuftubus
fumptibus et expenfis fuis propriis quod-

App.
IV.

dam

dam collegium perpetuum de uno cuſtode et ſcholaribus in Oxoniâ ac in uni-
verſitate ibidem ad ſtudendum et orandum
pro ſalubri ſtatu noſtro et ipſius compatris noſtri dum vixerimus, et animabus
noſtris cum ab hac luce migraverimus,
ac animabus clariſſimi principis Henrici
nuper regis Angliæ patris noſtri, Thomæ nuper ducis Clarenciæ avunculi noſtri, ducum, comitum, baronum, militum, armigerorum et aliorum nobilium
et ſubditorum ipſius patris noſtri et noſ-
trorum, qui temporibus et obſequiis ipſius patris noſtri et noſtri in guerris
regni Franciæ vitam finierunt, et animabus omnium fidelium defunctorum juxta
ordinationem ipſius compatris noſtri et
ſucceſſorum ſuorum fundare facere et
erigere dignaremur : nos ſupplicationi-
bus ejuſdem compatris noſtri annuentes,
in honore Domini noſtri Jeſu Chriſti,
gloriofiſſimæ

gloriofiffimæ Virginis Beatæ Mariæ ma-
tris ejus, et omnium fanctorum, Dei,
quoddam collegium perpetuum, fecundum harum feriem regendum, de uno
cuftode et viginti fcholaribus in dictâ
villâ Oxoniæ et univerfitate ejufdem
manfuris, ad ftudendum et orandum pro
falubri ftatu noftro et ipfius compatris
noftri dum vixerimus, et pro animabus
noftris cum ab hac luce migraverimus,
ac animabus ipfius clariffimi principis
patris noftri, Thomæ nuper ducis Clarenciæ avunculi noftri, ducum, comitum, baronum, militum, armigerorum
et fubditorum prædictorum, et animabus
omnium fidelium defunctorum, fuper
quoddam meffuagium vocatum Berford
Hall nuper vocatum Charleftonfyn, fex
fhopas et unam plateam vacuam eifdem
annexam in Oxoniâ, fuper quoddam cor-
nerum ex appofito finis orientalis ecclefiæ

fiæ parochialis Beatæ Mariæ Virginis, in vicis vocatis. Catſtrete et Seint Mary's ſtreet, continentibus longitudinem centum ſeptuaginta duorum pedum et latitudinem centum ſexaginta duorum pedum, quæ ordinatione ipſius compatris noſtri nuper habuimus ex conceſſione Thomæ Chichele archidiaconi Cantuariæ, Henrici Penwortham clerici, et Roberti Danvers feoffatorum, inde ad uſum præfati compatris noſtri habendum et tenendum nobis et hæredibus noſtris in perpetuum, pro hujuſmodi collegio ſuper eis conſtruendo, de aſſenſu ipſius compatris noſtri, quem ad ſucceſſores ſuos Cantuariæ archi-epiſcopos ob piam intentionem ſuam ac nonnullos ejus cuſtus ſumptus et expenſas, quos circa erectionem fundationem et dotationem ejuſdem collegii fecit et facere proponit in futurum, tanquam alteros fundatores ejuſdem collegii nominari

minari volentes, erigimus, ac tenore præfentium fundamus, facimus et ftabilimus,
perpetuis temporibus duraturum : Ac
Ricardum Andrewe clericum cuftodem
et pro cuftode ipfius collegii, et Thomam
Lavenham, Thomam Vange, Thomam
Wynterbourn, Robertum Hoo, Thomam
Lay, Ricardum Letofte, Willielmum
Horneden, Johannem Gygour, Johannem
Porter, Walterum Hert, Robertum Kar-
rewe, Simonem Hoore, Johannem Ju-
lyan, Walterum Hopton, Robertum
Stephens, Robertum Seborgh, Willielmum Overton, Thomam Efton, Richardum Warde, et Richardum Penwortham, fcholares refiduos ejufdem
collegii, per ipfum compatrem noftrum
electos et ad hoc affumptos, fecundum
ordinationes et ftatuta ipfius compatris
noftri et fuccefforum fuorum archiepif-
coporum Cantuariæ regendos, corrigendos,

dos, privandos et ammovendos præfeci-
mus creavimus et ordinavimus, præfici-
mus creamus et ordinamus per præfentes.
Volentes et concedentes, quod ipfe cuftos,
et fucceffores fui cuftodes ejufdem collegii, fecundum ordinationes et ftatuta prædicta eligere, congregare et admittere
poterit fibi plures fcholares ufque ad numerum quadraginta perfonarum, fecundum ordinationes et ftatuta prædicta
regendos, corrigendos privandos et ammovendos quos et fucceffores fuos fic
electos, congregatos et admiffos tanquam
fcholares et membra ejufdem collegii
fecundum prædicta ordinationes et ftatuta
regendos, corrigendos, privandos et ammovendos, pro nobis et hæredibus noftris
volumus et concedimus per præfentes ;
ita quod, decedente prædicto cuftode, cedente, vel eo quâcunque de caufâ inde
amoto feu privato, fcholares refidui
ejufdem

ejufdem collegii pro tempore ibidem exiftentes, fecundum formam et effectum ftatutorum et ordinationum prædictorum, alterum idoneum in cuftodem et pro cuftode ejufdem collegii eligant et eligere poffint, quem in cuftodem et pro cuftode ejufdem collegii per dominum compatrem noftrum et fucceffores fuos Cantuariæ archi-epifcopos, et non per nos, neque hæredes noftros, admitti et confirmari, fecundum ordinationes et ftatuta prædicta regendum, corrigendum, privandum et amovendum tenore præfentium duximus concedendum : et fic decedentibus hujufmodi cuftodibus, cedentibus; aut eis quoquo modo exinde privatis aut amotis, in futurum dicti fcholares collegii antedicti habeant et habere poffint, juxta ordinationes et ftatuta prædicta, liberam electionem de novis cuftodibus, quos, ut fupra dictum eft, admitti,

admitti, confirmari, regendos corrigendos' privandos et amovendos, et eos ſic in cuſtodes electos, admiſſos, confirmatos, regendos ut præfertur, cuſtodes eſſe perpetuos ejuſdem collegii, abſque licentiâ de nobis vel hæredibus noſtris inde petendâ ſeu proſequendâ, et non alios neque alio modo volumus et concedimus pro nobis et hæredibus noſtris, quantum in nobis eſt, in perpetuum. Volentes etiam quod decedentibus vel cedentibus ſcholaribus collegii antedicti, ſeu eorum aliquo decedente vel cedente, aut eis vel eorum aliquo exinde privatis vel amotis, privato vel amoto in futurum ſember habeant dictus cuſtos et ſucceſſores ſui prædicti in perpetuum, juxta ordinationes et ſtatuta prædicta liberam electionem, admiſſionem et confirmationem de novis ſcholaribus in eorum loco ponendis ; quos ſic electos, admiſſos et confir-' matos,

matos, abſque licentiâ inde de nobis vel hæredibus noſtris petendâ vel proſequendâ in futurum, et non alios tanquam ſcholares et membra eſſe ejuſdem collegii ſecundum ordinationes et ſtatuta prædicta regendos, corrigendos, privandos et amovendos volumus et concedimus pro nobis et hæredibus noſtris in perpetuum. Volentes ulterius quod cuſtos et ſcholares antedicti pro tempore ibidem degentes, et eorum ſucceſſores in perpetuum, Cuſtos et Collegium Animarum omnium Fidelium defunctorum de Oxoniâ nuncupentur. Et ulterius volumus et concedimus, quod cuſtos et ſcholares collegii antedicti ſimul pro tempore exiſtentes, et ſucceſſores ſui, per nomen vel ſub nomine cuſtodis et Collegii Animarum omnium fidelium defunctorum de Oxoniâ ſint perſonæ habiles, capaces et perpetuæ ad impetrandum, recipiendum, et ad inqui-

rendum

rendum terras, tenementa, redditus, fer-
vitia, proficua, advocationes ecclefiarum,
emolumenta, jura et poffeffiones tempo-
ralia et fpiritualia tam de nobis et hæredibus noftris quam de aliis perfonis
quibufcunque, licet ea immediate de
nobis et hæredibus noftris per fervitium
militare aut alio modo quocunque teneantur habendum, et tenendum eifdem
cuftodi et collegio et fuccefforibus fuis
in perpetuum. Et quod idem cuftos et
collegium et eorum fucceffores in perpetuum habeant unum figillum commune
pro negotiis et agendis fuis ferviturum.
Et quod ipfi et fucceffores fui per nomen prædictum implacitare poffint et
implacitari, et profequi omni modas caufas querelas et actiones reales perfonales
et mixtas cujufcunque generis fint vel
naturæ, et ad refpondendum vel defen-
dendum in eifdem coram judicibus fecu-
laribus

3

laribus et ecclefiafticis quibufcunque. Et ulterius damus et concedimus pro nobis et hæredibus noftris dictis cuftodi et collegio et fuccefforibus fuis prædictis dicta meffuagium fhopas et plateam, tam pro capellâ dicti collegii ac aliis domibus et ædificiis eidem neceffariis, quam pro eorum manfis et aliis neceffariis in et fuper eis conftruendis, habendum et tenendum eifdem cuftodi et collegio et fuccefforibus fuis in liberam puram et perpetuam elemofynam in perpetuum. Et infuper, ad effectum quod fcholares dicti collegii in eruditionibus fuis ac piis eorum orationibus melius manu teneri valeant et fuftentari, conceffimus et licentiam dedimus pro nobis et hæredibus noftris quantum in nobis eft præfato archiepifcopo et fuccefforibus fuis prædictis, quod ipfi, per affenfum prioris et capituli ecclefiæ Chrifti Cantuariæ pro

tempore

A P P. IV.

tempore exiftentes, advocationem et pa= tronatum ecclefiæ parochialis de Trenge Lincolnienfis diocefeos de provinciâ Cantuariæ, quæ eft de advocatione et patronatu ipfius compatris noftri, ut de jure archiepifcopatus fui Cantuarienfis prædicti, et quæ de nobis tenetur in ca= pite ut dicitur, eifdem cuftodi et collegio et fuccefforibus fuis dare poffint et af= fignare, habendum et tenendum præfatis cuftodi et collegio et fuccefforibus fuis in perpetuum, et eifdem cuftodi et colle= gio et fuccefforibus fuis prædictis, quod ipfi patronatum et advocationem prædic= tam a præfato archiepifcopo et fucceffo= ribus fuis prædictis in formâ prædictâ recipere, et ecclefiam illam appropriare, et eam fic appropriatam in proprios ufus tenere poffint fibi et fuccefforibus fuis prædictis in perpetuum: provifo femper quod vicaria ejufdem ecclefiæ, fecundum

ordinationem

ordinationem loci illius diocefani fuffi-
cienter dotetur, et quod quædam com-
petens fumma argenti inter pauperes
parochianos ejufdem ecclefiæ fingulis
annis diftribuatur, juxta formam ftatuti
inde editi et provifi. Et ulterius, de u-
beriori gratiâ noftrâ conceffimus et licentiam dedimus, pro nobis et hæredibus
noftris quantum in nobis eft, eifdem
cuftodi et collegio et fuccefforibus fuis
prædictis, quod ipfi et fucceffores fui
perquirere poffint terras et tenementa ad
valorem trecentarum librarum per annum, tam de terris et tenementis quæ
tam de nobis in capite quam de aliis
tenentur, habenda et tenenda eifdem
cuftodi et collegio et fuccefforibus fuis
prædictis, pro fuftentatione et eorum vic-
tu et veftitu ac aliis neceffariis eorum
agendis in perpetuum: dum tamen per

P   inquifitiones

A P P.
IV.

inquifitiones inde in formâ debitâ capi-
endas, et in cancellariam noftram et hære-
dum noftrorum rite retornandas, comper-
tum exiftat, quod fieri poffit abfque
damno vel prejudicio noftro vel hære-
dum noftrorum, aut alicujus alterius cujufcunque: et quod expreffa mentio de
valore eorundem meffuagii, fhopparum et
plateæ minime facta eft, feu ftatuti de
terris ac tenementis ad manum mortuam
non ponendis; feu quod prædicta advo-
catio et patronatus de nobis, ut præfertur,
tenentur in capite, feu aliquo alio ftatuto
five ordinatione in contrarium factum
edito, non obftante. Et hoc abfque aliquo
feodo magno feu parvo, aut alio fine quocunque nobis aut hæredibus noftris reddendo vel faciendo pro præmiffis, vel
aliquo præmifforum. Et ulterius de gratiâ noftrâ fpeciali, pro nobis et hæredibus
noftris

hoſtris quantum in nobis eſt, relaxamus
eiſdem cuſtodi et collegio et ſucceſſoribus ſuis in perpetuum omnimoda corro-
dia, penſiones, annuitates, et alia quæcunque, quæ nos vel hæredes noſtri, aut
aliquis alius ad noſtrum rogatum aut
mandatum, nomine fundationis noſtræ
antedictæ, ab eiſdem cuſtode et collegio
et ſucceſſoribus ſuis prædictis exigere
poſſumus aut poſſint in futurum; et eos
inde quietos eſſe volumus et concedimus,
per præſentes perpetuis temporibus du-
raturas. Et ulterius, de uberiori gratiâ
noſtrâ conceſſimus eiſdem cuſtodi et
collegio et ſucceſſoribus ſuis in perpetuum, quod quotieſcunque et quando-
cunque collegium illud futuris temporibus de cuſtode, per mortem, ceſſionem,
privationem, ſeu reſignationem, aut alio
modo quocunque, vacare contigerit, reſi-

dui

dui scholares ejusdem collegii pro tempore ibidem existentes habeant et percipiant omnimodos fructus, proficua et emolumenta, de terris, tenementis, reddibus, servitiis, et rectoriis et aliis possessionibus quibuscunque ejusdem collegii, seu eidem collegio spectantibus, durante hujusmodi vacatione provenientia, secundum ordinationes et statuta prædicta disponenda, quæ tempore et ratione hujusmodi vacationis ad nos vel hæredes nostros pertinent seu pertinere poterunt in futurum, absque computo seu aliquo alio nobis vel hæredibus nostris inde reddendo. Itaque nos et hæredes nostri ab omni custodiâ, seisina, seu possessione ejusdem collegii, aut terrarum, tenementorum, reddituum, servitiorum, rectoriarum, et aliarum possessionum quarumcunque ejusdem collegii, seu eidem spectantium,

durante

durante hujufmodi vacatione, fimus ex-
clufi in perpetuum per præfentes. In
cujus rei teftimonium has literas noftras
fieri fecimus patentes, Tefte meipfo apud
manerium noftrum de Kenyngton, vice-
fimo die Maii, anno regni noftri fexto-
decimo.

Wymbyfh.

Per breve de privato figillo.

APPENDIX, N°V.

Bulla Eugenii.

EUGENIUS epifcopus, fervus fervorum Dei, ad perpetuam rei memoriam, ex injuncto nobis defuper apoftolicæ fervitutis officio ad ea libenter intendimus, per quæ ecclefiæ et capellæ ac alia ecclefiaftica loca quælibet, præfertim ad ufum dedit fcientiæ litterarum, per quam augmentatur et crefcit religio fidei Chriftianæ, multiplicari valeant, ac in illis majeftas Altiffimi etiam ad fidelium animarum falutem in gratiarum benedictionibus collaudetur, fúique cultus gloriofi nominis amplietur;

6

amplietur; nuper fiquidem ad fupplica-
tionem venerabilis fratris noftri Henrici
Chichele, archiepifcopi Cantuarienfis, totius Angliæ primatis, et apoftolicæ fedis
legati, erectionem et fundationem cujuf-
dam collegii Animarum omnium fidelium defunctorum nuncupati, in villâ
Oxonienfi, Lincolnienfi diocefi, in quâ
litterarum ftudium viget generale, de bonis dicti archiepifcopi tunc conftrui et
ædificari laudabiliter inchoati et in parte
dotati, pro uno cuftode et quadraginta
pauperibus fcholaribus dictis, per cariffimum in Chrifto filium noftrum Henri-
cùm regem Angliæ illuftrem tunc factas
ex certâ fcientiâ confirmavimus, aliaque
fecimus prout in noftris defuper confec-
tis literis plenius continetur. Nos igitur, ut in dicto collegio cultus divinus
ad Altiffimi laudem et gloriam, necnon
fidelium animarum falutem, dictique col-

legii

legii confervationem et ftatum falubrem, continuo vigeat, quantum cum Deo poffumus providere, volentes archiepifcopi præfati, qui alter, cum dicto rege, fundator et patronus exiftit, in hac parte fupplicationibus inclinari, fibi et cuftodi pro tempore exiftenti, ac præfentibus et futuris fociis et fcholaribus dicti collegii, auctoritate apoftolicâ tenore præfentium. Concedimus pariter et indulgemus, quod ipfi unam capellam feu oratorii domum pro miffis et aliis divinis officiis inibi celebrandis et audiendis, necnon unum cimiterium pro eorum ac etiam præfentium et futurorum ipfius collegii prefbyterorum, clericorum, familiarium, fervientium, miniftrorum, et perfonarum pro tempore decedentium, corporibus tumulandis, infra fepta prædicti collegii, in locis tamen ad hoc congruis et honeftis, conftruere, erigere et ordinare, feu conftrui, erigi et ordinari,

ordinari, ipfamque capellam per quem- A ꝑ ꝓ.
cunque maluerint catholicum antiftitem, V.
gratiam et communionem apoftolicæ fedis habentem, dedicare feu facere confe-
crari, ac in eâ tunc conftructâ et confe-
cratâ, quotiefcunque de cætero villam
prædictam ecclefiaftico interdicto fupponi
forfan contigerit, claufis januis, excom-
municatis et interdictis exclufis, non
pulfatis campanis, fubmiffâ voce per fe ac
prædictos aliofque idoneos prefbyteros
ac clericos, in fuâ, ac etiam præfentium
et futurorum familiarium, fervientium,
miniftrorum et perfonarum eorundem,
præfentiâ, dummodo ipfi vel illi caufam
interdicto non dederunt, nec id eis vel illis
fpecialiter interdici contigerit, miffas et
officia hujufmodi celebrare et celebrari facere; ipfique cuftos pro tempore, ac præfentes et futuri focii, fcholares, prefbyteri,
clerici, familiares, miniftri, fervientes, et
perfonæ

personæ omnes et singuli, etiam absque or-
dinarii loci, necnon præpositi et sociorum
aulæ regalis, ac vicarii parochialis ecclesiæ
Beatæ Mariæ ejusdem villæ, infra cujus ecclesiæ parochialis metas collegium hujusmodi confistit, pro tempore existentium,
et aliorum quorumlibet consensu seu licentiâ, tam interdictis hujusmodi, quam
aliis quibuslibet temporibus ac diebus,
easdem missas et officia in capellâ seu
oratorii domo hujusmodi audire, et, quoties expediens fuerit, a singulis sacerdotibus idoneis, ad id per ipsum custodem de
numero sociorum scholarium vel presby-
terorum prædictorum præsentium et futurorum, seu alias pro tempore eligendis
ac deputandis, eucaristicæ, olei sancti, ac
alia sacramentalia et ecclesiastica quæcunque recipere; necnon idem pro tempore
custos sacerdotes præfatos ad sacramenta
et sacramentalia hujusmodi, ut præmitti-
tur,

tur, miniftranda quoties oportuerit eligere
ac deputare; capellam infuper feu domum
præfatam, quoties illam per fanguinis
effufionem, aut feminis pollutionem, vel
alias quomodolibet violari contigerit, per
fe vel alium facerdotem idoneum, quem
duxerit, eligendum, aquâ, prius per fimi-
lem antiftitem, eandem gratiam et com-
muniónem habentem, ut moris eft, be-
nedictâ reconciliare, ipfique facerdotes
facramenta vel alia facramentalia hujufmodi ut præfertur miniftrare perpetuis
futuris temporibus libere et licite valeant atque poffint. Rurfus eifdem auctoritate ac tenore ftatuimus decernimus
et ordinamus, quod de cætero ullo unquam tempore cuftos, focii collegii, fcholares, clerici, fervientes, miniftri, et perfonæ præfentes et futuri hujufmodi, feu
aliquis ex eis, miffas vel alia divina officia
in dictâ ecclefiâ audire, feu illis inibi
interefte,

interesse, aut sacramenta et sacramentalia hujusmodi ab aliis quam a præfatis pro tempore electis sacerdotibus suscipere, seu oblationes vel contributiones quascunque præposito aut sociis aulæ, vel vicario, prædictis facere seu exhibere, aut alia onera quæcunque et qualiacunque supportare, quavis ratione, occasione, vel causâ, minime teneantur, nec ad id per præpositum, socios aulæ, et vicarium, prædictos, vel eorum aliquem aut alium quemcunque inviti compelli possint. Præterea quod omnia et singula oblationes, obventiones, legata, relicta et donata, ac alia emolumenta quæcunque, in quibusvis bonis mobilibus et immobilibus, ac pecuniis et rebus aliis illa consistant, tam ratione custodis, sociorum collegii, scholarium, familiarium, servientium, et ministrorum præsentium et futurorum prædictorum, quam alias quo-

3.   modolibet

modolibet eifdem capellæ feu domui A ? p.
collegio proventura, abfque eo quod il- V.
lorum vel alicujus eorum media feu
quarta aut alia quæcunque pars præpo-
fito, fociis aulæ, ecclefiæ et vicario, prædictis, vel aliis quibufvis locis feu perfonis, aut eorum alicui, etiam fi illa eis
de jure vel confuetudine forfan tunc
debita fuerit, perfolvatur feu affignetur,
aut folvi vel affignari debeat, ad collegium et capellam feu domum, nec non
cuftodem pro tempore, ac præfentes ac
futuros focios collegii, et fcholares hujufmodi, integre et cum effectu fpectent
et pertineant, ac fpectare et pertinere
debeant, de illifque cuftos pro tempore,
focii collegii, et fcholares hujufmodi,
libere difponere, ac ea in fuos et dicti
collegii ufus utilitatemque convertere
poffint, ex nunc eofdem cuftodem pro
tempore, ac præfentes et futuros focios
collegii,

collegii, fcholares, clericos, miniftros, fervientes, et perfonas a miffarum divino-
rumque in dicta ecclefiâ auditione, feu
illis inibi intereffentia, ac facramentorum
et facramentalium fufceptione, nec non
oblationum feu contributionum exhibi-
tione onerumque fupportatione, ac mediæ
feu quartæ vel alterius partis folutione
feu affignatione hujufmodi auctoritate
præfata harum   plenarie eximentes,
et totaliter liberantes, nec non decernen-
tes omnes et fingulos proceffus quofcun-
que, excommunicationis, fufpenfionis,
et interdicti, aliafque fententias, cenfuras
et pænas in fe continentes, quos et quas
ac quicquid contra tenorem præfentium
forfan haberi feu fulminari contigerit,
irrita et inania exiftere, nulliufque ro-
boris vel momenti ; non obftantibus fe-
licis recordationis Clementis   et pre-
deceffioris noftri, et aliis apoftolicis, nec

non

non bonæ memoriæ Ottonis et Ottoboni, olim in regno Angliæ fedis apoftolicæ legatorum, ac in generalibus, provincialibus et finodalibus conciliis editis, conftitutionibus et ordinationibus, ftatutis quoque et confuetudinibus localibus cæterifque contrariis quibufcunque. Nulli ergo omnino hominum liceat hanc paginam noftrorum conceffionis, ftatuti, conftitutionis, ordinationis et liberationis, infringere, vel ei aufu temerario contra-ire. Si quis autem hoc attemptare præfumpferit, indignationem omnipotentis Dei, et beatorum Petri et Pauli apoftolorum ejus fe noverit incurfurum. Dat. Florentiæ, anno incarnationis Domini millefimo quadrageffimo triceffimo-nono, undecimo kalendarum Julii, pontificatus noftri anno nono.

Poggius.

APPENDIX,

APPENDIX, Nº VI.

A Lift of the Purchafes and Grants made for the original Site of the College.

*B*ERFORD HALL, purchafed of John Brome fenior and John Brome junior, of Warwick, by Thomas Chichelé, Henry Penwortham, and Robert Danvers, 14th of December, 16th of Henry VI; and granted by the king to the college 20th of May following.

Skibbowe's Tenement, in the High ftreet, purchafed of Roger Skibbowe by Thomas Chichelé, John Birkhede, John Bold,

Bold, and Robert Danvers, 4th of July, 16th of Henry VI; made over by them to Henry VI. 13th of January, 20th of his reign; and granted by the king to the college 24th of April in the fame year. It formerly belonged to the monaftery of St. John of Scyreburne; and the referved rent then paid to that monaftery has fince, I believe, been paid to Univerfity college.

Between this tenement and Berford Hall two tenements intervened, *one* belonging to the convent of St. Fridefwide, the *other* to a chantry of St. Mary's church. The former, which joined Berford Hall, was granted by that convent to the college, under a referved annual rent, now payable to the dean and chapter of Chrift Church, by a deed dated 11th of September, 21ft of Henry VI.:

Q   the

the latter, which belonged to Oriel college, was granted by that fociety to the college of All Souls under a fmall referved rent, 1ft of November, 22d of Henry VI.

St. Thomas's Hall, in Cat-ftreet, fituated next to Berford Hall, granted to the college by the convent of Ofney, 11th of September, 21ft of Henry VI. referving an annual rent, now payable to the dean and chapter of Chrift Church : it was the fite of the chapel, as the deed fpecifies, " fuper quod tenementum ca-
" pella collegii antedicti ædificatur."

To the north of this, in the fame ftreet, was *Berford's Tenement* ; it was purchafed of Joan the widow, and John the fon of John Berford, by Thomas Chichelé, John Birkhede, John Druell, and

3   Robert

Robert Danvers, 5th May, 17th of Henry VI. conveyed by them to the king 13th of January; and granted by the king to the college 24th of April, 20th of his reign.

Tyngfwick Inn, early alienated by Nicholas de Tyngſwyck to the univerſity, and granted by them to the college about the year 1440; as the rationarium fundationis, ſo often quoted before, mentions a reſerved rent paid for it to the univerſity in that year, " Solut. univer- " ſit. pro tenem. vocat. Tyngſwick " Inn."

Next to this was a *tenement* belonging to the convent of St. Fridefwyde, and purchaſed under one deed, together with another tenement in High-ſtreet, mentioned before, 11th September, 21ſt of

Q 2   Henry

APP. VI. Henry VI. upon which two tenements, as the deed expreſſes, a part of the college was then built; " Super quæ duo " tenementa parcella collegii *modo* con- " ſtituitur et fundatur."

THESE ſeveral tenements contained the original ſite of the college, and were all either rented or purchaſed at the time of the foundation.

From MS. abſtract of charters made by order of Gilbert Sheldon, warden in 1640.

APPENDIX,

APPENDIX, N° VII.

THE ſtone employed in the build- A p p.
ings of the college was brought VII.
from the quarries of Hedington, Teynton, Sherborn, Henxey, and Sunningwell. The woods of Shotover, Stow-
wood, Horſham, Eynſham, Cumner,
and Beckley ſupplied the timber: of
which

Without particularly marking the references, I
ſhall give the following entries from the *Rationarium fundationis*, in the ſame order in which they
are alluded to in the text.

" Lapides empti apud Edyngdon, Teynton,
" Sherborn, Sunningwell, Henxey."

" Pro proſtratione arborum in Schottore et Stou-
" wode, pro 3 acris meremii querc. empt. in ne-
" more de Horſham, pro 6 peciis merem. querc.
" empt.

which the king prefented the archbifhop with twelve trees from his park
of Beckley, and the abbot of Abingdon
twenty from Cumner.

THE workmen were the ableſt that
could be procured. Maſons were hired
in the fourth year of the building of the
college, from London, and the diſtant
counties of Norfolk and Suffolk : who
appear to have been well-ſkilled in their
art, ſince they were ſoon ſent for by the
king's mandate, to aſſiſt in repairing his
caſtle

" empt. in quodam nemore juxtà Eynſham. Pro
" cariagio de 20 arbor. de dono de abbat. de Abyng-
" don in nemore de Cumpnore. Pro cariagio de
" 12 arbor. dat. per regem in parco de Beckley.".

" Pro expenſis lathomiorum venient. a London,
" pro expenſis lathomiorum venient. a Northfolciâ
" et Southfolciâ : ad cariandum harneſ. lathomior.
" uſque ad Wyndſore per mandatum regis arreſta-
" torum ad ejus reparationem."

" Solut.

caſtle of Windſor. The wages of the
different perſons occupied in carrying on this work, were, to carpenters and ſawyers, ſix pence a day—maſons, eight pence—ſtone-diggers and common labourers, four pence halfpenny—joiners, from ſix pence to eight pence—dawber, five pence — maſter - carpenter, three ſhillings and four pence a-week—carvers and image makers, four ſhillings and eight pence a-week, bed and board found them. A woman-labourer, three pence a-day. The windows were glazed at one ſhilling a-foot.

FROM

" Solut. carpentariis ſingulis capient. per diem
" 6 d. Solut. farratorib. ſing. capient. per diem 6 d.
" Solut. operariis ſing. cap. per diem 4¼ d. Solut.
" latomiis per diem 8 d. Solut. lapifodiatori per
" diem 4¼ d. Solut. egidio joynor per diem 8 d.
" alio joynor per diem 6 d. Solut. Johanni Marche
" dawber per diem 5 d. Solut. J. Branch carpent.
" princip. per ebdomad. 3 s. 4 d. Solut. John.
" Maſſyngham

From this detail of the wages of the mechanic and the labourer, at the period under confideration, they will appear to have been, after allowing for the decreafe of value in money, both from the diminution in the coin, and the great influx of fpecie fince that period, nearly double of what they are at prefent.

" Maffyngham factori imaginum, et kerver, cap.
" per ebdom. 4 s. 8 d. Solut. mulieri 3 d. per
" diem. Solut. Johanni Glafier locato per domin.
" contuas. ad vitrandum 8 feneftras in corpore ca-
" pellæ : ad vitrand. unam feneftram in ftudio gar-
" diani, ad vitrandum 6 feneftras, minores in navi
" capellæ *per pedem quadratum* 12 d."

F I N I S.